"Everyone has their price, Mr. Doukakis."

"You think so?" Intrigued, Damon allowed his gaze to drop to the creamy skin visible at the neck of her formal white shirt. "So what's your price, Miss Prince?"

"I was talking about business."

Damon smiled. "Of course you were. Someone with your exceptional morals would never become tangled with someone like me, would they?"

His sarcasm brought a scarlet tinge to her cheeks but she didn't defend herself. "Have you finished?"

"Finished?" Damon slowly lifted his gaze and stared down into those eyes. They were the blue of a summer sky. "I haven't even started."

21st CENTURY
BOSSES

Impossible, infuriating and utterly irresistible!

In the high-octane world of international business, these arrogant yet devastatingly attractive men reign supreme.

On his speed dial, at his beck and call 24/7, it takes a special kind of woman to cope with this boss's outrageous demands!

Look out for more in 2012!

Sarah Morgan

DOUKAKIS'S APPRENTICE

TORONTO NEW YORK LONDON
AMSTERDAM PARIS SYDNEY HAMBURG
STOCKHOLM ATHENS TOKYO MILAN MADRID
PRAGUE WARSAW BUDAPEST AUCKLAND

Recycling programs
for this product may
not exist in your area.

ISBN-13: 978-0-373-13021-4

DOUKAKIS'S APPRENTICE

First North American Publication 2011

Printed in U.S.A.

All about the author...
Sarah Morgan

USA TODAY bestselling author **SARAH MORGAN** writes lively, sexy stories for both the Harlequin Presents and Medical Romance lines.

As a child, Sarah dreamed of being a writer and although she took a few interesting detours on the way, she is now living that dream. With her writing career, she has successfully combined business with pleasure and she firmly believes that reading romance is one of the most satisfying and fat-free escapist pleasures available. Her stories are unashamedly optimistic and she is always pleased when she receives letters from readers saying that her books have helped them through hard times.

RT Book Reviews has described her writing as "action packed and sexy" and has nominated her books for its Reviewers' Choice Award and "Top Pick" slot.

Sarah lives near London with her husband and two children, who innocently provide an endless supply of authentic dialogue. When she isn't writing or reading, Sarah enjoys music, movies and any activity that takes her outdoors.

Readers can find out more about Sarah and her books from her website, www.sarahmorgan.com. She can also be found on Facebook and Twitter.

Books by Sarah Morgan

Harlequin Presents®
3000—A NIGHT OF SCANDAL *(The Notorious Wolfes)*
2970—BELLA AND THE MERCILESS SHEIKH
 (The Balfour Brides)
2943—ONE NIGHT...NINE-MONTH SCANDAL

CHAPTER ONE

'HE'S here. He's arrived. Damon Doukakis just strode into the building.'

Woken by the panicky voice, Polly lifted her head from her arms and was blinded by sunlight pouring through the window. 'What? Who?' The words were slurred, her brain emerging slowly from the shadows of sleep. The headache that had been part of her life for the past week still squeezed her skull. 'I must have dozed off. Why didn't anyone wake me?'

'Because you haven't slept for days and you're scary when you're tired. There's no need to panic. I'm doing that for both of us. Here—I brought sustenance.' Balancing two mugs of and a large muffin, the woman kicked the door shut. 'Wake yourself up with carbs and coffee.'

Polly rubbed her eyes and squinted at the screen of her laptop. 'What time is it?'

'Eight o'clock.'

'Eight o'clock?' She flew to her feet, sending papers and pens spinning across the floor. 'The meeting is in fifteen minutes! Were you hoping I'd just walk in there and talk in my sleep or something?' Polly hit 'save' on the document she'd been working on all night, her hand shaking from the sudden awakening. Her heart pounded and deep in her stomach was a solid lump of dread.

Sleeping didn't make any of it go away and reality pressed down on her like a heavy weight.

Everything was about to change. Life as she knew it had ended.

'Stay calm,' Debbie swooped across the office and put the plate and the mugs on the desk. 'If you show him you're afraid, he'll walk all over you. That's what men like Damon Doukakis do. They sniff out weakness and they move in for the kill.'

'I'm not afraid.' The lie wedged itself in her throat.

She *was* afraid. She was afraid of the responsibility and of the consequences of failure. And, yes, she was afraid of Damon Doukakis.

Only a fool wouldn't be.

'You're going to be fine. I mean, we're all depending on you, *obviously,* but I don't want the fact that you have the future of a hundred people in your hands to make you nervous.'

'Thanks for that calming thought.' Polly allowed herself a quick gulp of coffee and then checked her BlackBerry. 'I've only been asleep for two hours and I already have a hundred e-mails. Don't these people ever sleep?' She scrolled through them quickly, scanning for anything important. 'Gérard Bonnel wants us to move our meeting tomorrow back to the evening. Can I get a later flight to Paris?'

'You're not flying. The train was cheaper. I bought you a non-flexible ticket on the seven-thirty out of St Pancras. If he's moved the meeting then you'll have most of the day to kill.' Debbie leaned forward and stole a large chunk from the muffin. 'Go and see the Eiffel Towel. Make love to a delicious French guy on the banks of the Seine. *Ooh la la.*'

In the process of replying to an e-mail, Polly didn't look up. 'Public sex is an offence, even in France.'

'Nowhere near as big an offence as your non-existent sex-life. When did you last go on a date?'

'I have enough problems without adding a sex-life to the

mix.' Polly pressed 'send'. 'Did you sort out a purchase order for that magazine promotion?'

'Yes, yes. Do you ever stop thinking about work? The fearsome Damon Doukakis just might have met his match in you.'

'The rest of these e-mails are going to have to wait.' Polly put the phone down on her desk and glanced at the clock. 'Damn—I wanted to take another look at the presentation. I need to brush my hair—I don't know what to do first—'

'Hair. You slept with your head on your arms and you look like Mohican Barbie.' Debbie whipped a pair of hair straighteners out of Polly's drawer and plugged them in. 'Hold still. This is an emergency.'

'I need to go to the bathroom and do my make up.'

'No time. Don't worry. You look great. I *love* that look. You're so good at mixing vintage with current.' Debbie slid the irons down Polly's hair. 'The hot pink tights really work.'

Keeping her head still, Polly reached out and unplugged her laptop. 'I can't believe my dad still hasn't rung. His company is being decimated and he's nowhere in sight. I've left about a hundred messages.'

'You know he never switches his mobile on. He hates the thing. There—' Debbie unplugged the irons '—you're done.'

Polly twisted her hair and pinned it in a haphazard knot at the back of her head. 'I even called a few of the London hotels last night to see if a middle-aged gentleman and a young woman had rented a suite with them.'

'That must have been embarrassing.'

'I grew up with embarrassing.' She retrieved her boots from under the desk. 'Damon Doukakis is going to rip us apart when he realises my father isn't showing up.'

'The rest of us will make up for it. The whole company came in early. We're all busy bees. If Doukakis is looking for slackers, he's not going to find them here. We're determined to make a good impression despite your father's absence.'

'It's too late. Damon Doukakis has already made up his mind what he wants to do with us.' And she knew what that was. Panic gripped her. He'd taken control of her father's company. He could do anything he liked with the business.

It was his revenge. His way of sending a message to her father.

But it was a crude weapon. The scorching blaze of his wrath wasn't just going to burn up her father—it was going to burn up the innocent staff who didn't deserve to lose their jobs.

The weight of responsibility was suffocating. As her father's daughter she knew she had to do something, but in truth she was powerless. She had no authority.

Debbie ate a piece of muffin. 'I read somewhere that Damon Doukakis works a twenty-hour day so at least you'll have something in common.'

After three nights with virtually no sleep Polly could barely focus. Drugged by tiredness, she struggled to shake the clouds from her brain. 'I've put together the figures. Let's just hope Michael Anderson can work the laptop. You know what he's like with technology. I've backed up the entire presentation in three places because he managed to delete the thing last time. Are the rest of the board here?'

'They all arrived at the same time as him. Not that they said anything to us.' Deep lines of disapproval bracketed Debbie's mouth. 'None of them have the bottle to face us since they sold their shares to Demon Damon. I still don't understand why a rich, powerful tycoon like him would want to buy our little company. I mean, I love working here, but we're not exactly his style are we?'

Polly thought about how hard she'd worked to try and drag

the company into the twenty-first century. 'No. We're not his style.'

'So did he buy us for the fun of it?' Debbie finished the muffin and licked her fingers. 'Maybe this is billionaire retail therapy. Instead of buying shoes, he blows a fortune on an ad agency. He offered the board a whole heap of money.'

Polly kept her mouth shut but the dark dread turned to an icy chill.

She knew why he'd bought the company. And it wasn't something she could share with anyone. Damon Doukakis had sworn her to silence in a single chilling phone call that had come a few days earlier. A phone call she hadn't mentioned to anyone. She didn't want it to be public knowledge any more than he did.

Polly forced herself to breathe slowly. 'I'm not surprised the board sold. They're greedy. I'm so sick of booking their long lunches and their first-class airfares and then being told we're not profitable. They remind me of mosquitoes, sucking up our lifeblood into their fat bodies—'

Debbie recoiled. 'Pol, that's gross.'

'*They're* gross.' Polly mentally ran through everything she'd put into the presentation. Had she missed anything? 'If I were the one giving the presentation, I wouldn't be so worried.'

'You should be the one giving it.'

'Michael Anderson is too threatened by me to let me open my mouth. He's afraid I might actually tell someone who does the work around here. And anyway, I'm just my father's executive assistant, whatever that is. My job is to keep everything running behind the scenes.' And she was horribly conscious that she had no formal qualifications. She'd learned by watching, listening and trusting her instincts and she was savvy enough to know that for most employers that wouldn't be enough. Polly pressed her hands to her churning stomach, wishing she could stride into the boardroom wielding an MBA from Harvard. 'Doukakis already has a super-slick success-ful advertising agency in his organisation. He doesn't need another one and he doesn't need our staff. He's just going to snap his jaws around us like—'

'No!' Debbie held up her hand and shuddered. 'Don't tell me what it will be like. No more of your blood-sucking-mos-quito analogies—I just ate your breakfast.'

'I'm just saying—'

'Well, *don't* say. And if Damon Doukakis wants your fa-ther's business that badly, well—that's sort of a compliment, isn't it? And you're assuming he'll make us all redundant, but he might not. Why buy a business and then break it up?'

Because he wanted to be in control.

Instead of being a helpless passenger like her, Damon had put himself in the driving seat. While her father was living the life of a man half his age, his company was being savaged by a ruthless predator. And she was fighting that predator single-handed.

'Cheer up.' Debbie patted her shoulder. 'Damon Doukakis might not be as ruthless as they say. You've never actually met him in person.'

Oh, yes, she had.

Feeling her face turn the same colour as her tights, Polly closed her laptop.

They'd met just once, in the head's office the day she and one other girl had been permanently excluded from the ex-clusive girls' boarding school they attended. Unfortunately that one other girl had been his sister and Damon Doukakis had turned the full force of his anger and recrimination onto Polly, the ringleader.

Just thinking about that day was enough to make her body tremble like a leaf in the wind.

She was under no illusions about what the future held for her.

To Damon Doukakis she was a troublemaker with an attitude problem.

When he lifted his axe, she'd be the first for the chop.

Polly ran her hand over the back of her neck. Maybe she'd just offer to resign if he kept the staff on. He wanted a sacrifice for her father's behaviour, didn't he? So she'd be the sacrifice.

Debbie picked up the empty plate. 'So who *is* your dad seeing this time? Not that Spanish woman he met at Salsa classes?'

'No, I—I don't know.' The lie slid easily over her lips. 'I haven't asked.' Stressed out of her mind, Polly picked up her BlackBerry and slipped it into the pocket of her dress. 'It's crazy, isn't it? I can't believe that Damon Doukakis is about to stride in here and take away everything my dad has ever worked for and he is in some hotel somewhere—'

'—having wild monkey sex with a woman who is probably half his age?'

'Don't! I don't want to think about my father having sex, especially with a woman my age.' *Especially not this woman.*

'You should be used to it by now. Do you think your dad realises that his colourful sex-life has put you off ever having a relationship?'

'I don't have time for this conversation.' Blocking out thoughts of her father, Polly wriggled her feet into her boots and zipped them up. 'Have you arranged coffee and pastries for the boardroom?'

'All done. But Damon Doukakis is probably just going to feast on the staff. He's like a great white shark.' Adding to the aura of menace, Debbie made a fin with her hands and hummed the theme from *Jaws*. 'He glides through the smooth waters of commerce, eating everything that gets in his way. He's at the top of the food chain, whereas we're right at the bottom of the ocean. We're nothing more than plankton. Let's just hope we're too small to be a tasty snack.'

Uncomfortable with the analogy, Polly glanced protectively towards the fish tank that she kept on her desk. 'Keep your voice down. Romeo and Juliet are getting nervous. They're hiding behind the pond weed.' She wished she could join the fish. Never in her life had she ever dreaded anything as much as this meeting. Over the past few days she'd sacrificed sleep trying to put together a convincing case for saving the staff. She no longer had any illusions about her own future, but these people were like her family and she was going to fight to the death to protect them.

The phone on her desk rang and she picked it up with the same degree of enthusiasm a doomed man would display on his walk to the gallows. 'Polly Prince…' She recognised the slightly slurred tones of Michael Anderson, her father's deputy and the agency's creative director. Despite the hour, he'd obviously already had a drink. As he instructed her to bring the laptop to the boardroom, Polly gripped the phone tightly. *Snake.* The man hadn't had a creative idea for at least a decade. He'd bled the agency dry and now he'd sold his shares to Damon Doukakis for an inflated price.

Anger shot through her. If they hadn't sold out, this whole situation might have been contained.

Slamming down the phone, Polly scooped up her laptop, determined to do what she could to fight for the staff.

'Good luck.' Debbie glanced at Polly's feet. 'Wow. Those boots are perfect for kicking ass. And they make you look *tall.*'

'That's the idea.' Last time she'd met Damon Doukakis he'd made her feel small in every way. Physically and emotionally, he'd towered over her. It wasn't going to happen again. This time she was determined that when he glared at her they were going to be eye to eye.

Walking towards the boardroom felt like walking the plank. It didn't help that every two seconds someone stuck their head out of an office to wish her luck, each nervous smile making her more aware of the depth of her responsibility. They were relying on her, but deep down she knew she had no influence and virtually nothing with which to defend them. It was like going into battle armed only with her hairdryer. She was just hoping that Michael Anderson would use the presentation she'd put together to fight for them.

The doors to the boardroom were closed and she paused to draw breath, irritated by how nervous she was. Not of the board—for them she felt nothing but contempt—but of Damon Doukakis. She breathed out, slow and long, telling herself that ten years was a long time. Maybe the rumours were wrong. Maybe he'd developed a human streak.

She was relying on it.

Knocking briskly, she opened the door. For a moment all she saw were smug expressions, a litter of coffee cups and dark suits hugging bodies fattened by too many lunches.

The boys' club.

Still clutching her laptop, Polly forced herself to walk forward. As the doors were closed behind her she looked around the table at the men she'd worked with since she'd left school at eighteen. Not one of them looked her in the eye.

Bad sign, she thought grimly.

A couple of the directors stared at the notes in front of them. The atmosphere was thick with tension and anticipation. They reminded her of the bloodthirsty, voyeuristic crowds that sometimes gathered round the scene of an accident. To some, there was nothing so compelling as watching another human being in deep trouble. And she was in deep trouble. Knowing that every man around the table was now a millionaire several times over, Polly felt nothing but disgust.

They reminded her of a pack of hyenas ready to benefit from someone else's kill.

They'd sold her father out without hesitation.

And they'd sold out the staff.

She was so furious with the lot of them that it took her a moment to notice the man positioned at the head of the table.

Occupying her father's chair with arrogant assurance and no evidence of conscience, Damon Doukakis presided over the meeting like a conqueror surveying his captives. He didn't speak or move, but somehow everything about his body language screamed masculine aggression.

Her heart pumping, Polly placed the laptop carefully on the polished surface of the boardroom table.

Those dangerous black eyes watched her and she wondered how he could convey authority when he hadn't even opened his mouth. Somehow he dominated the room, his economy of movement and speech intensifying the aura of power that clung to him like a protective force field.

A superbly tailored suit skimmed his wide shoulders and a snowy white shirt dazzled against his bronzed throat. The knot of his tie was perfect—everything about him was sleek and impeccably groomed. He presented a startling contrast to the rest of the men around the table. Not for this man the excess weight that came with endless business entertaining. Under the expensive suit, his body was hard and strong—honed, no doubt, by exercise and the same rigid self-discipline he applied to his business practices.

Women found him irresistible, of course. He was pure alpha male, the controlling force behind one of the fastest-growing, most successful companies in Europe. In the darkening gloom of economic depression, the Doukakis Media Group was the bright star that shone the light of recovery.

It irritated Polly extremely that the man not only had a

towering intellect and an astonishing gift for business, he also looked that good. There was no justice, she thought savagely as she opened up her laptop and reminded herself not to be fooled by the sleek suit or the other outward trappings of civility. As far as she was concerned, the clothes did nothing to mask what he was—a ruthless opportunist who was willing to stop at nothing to achieve his chosen goal. But she understood why the board had sold out to him. He was the King of the beasts, she thought numbly, and the men around him were just lunch, to be consumed in one snap of his jaws. They were weak, and the weak would never challenge a man like Damon Doukakis any more than a wildebeest would turn on a lion.

Look him in the eye, Polly. Look him in the eye.

Knowing that the worst thing she could do was show him she was afraid, she looked. It was only for a second, but something passed between them. The impact of that wordless exchange slammed into her and she dragged her gaze away, shaking from head to toe. She'd expected to feel intimidated. What she hadn't expected was the flash of sexual awareness.

Shaken, Polly switched on the laptop, desperately hoping that he wasn't aware of her reaction to him.

'Gentlemen…' She paused. 'And Mr Doukakis.'

There was grim humour in the smile that played around the corners of his mouth and despite her best intentions Polly found herself staring at the sensual curve of his lips. According to rumour, sexual conquests came as easily to him as the business deals. Doukakis was as ruthless, unemotional and calculating in his relationships as he was in the other areas of his life. Maybe that was why he was so protective of his sister, she thought numbly. He knew what men were like.

But so did she. And an inconvenient flash of chemistry wasn't going to change her opinion.

As her eyes met his again, her tongue suddenly jammed against the roof of her mouth and her lips refused to form the words that had gathered in her brain. In that single moment she saw that he knew. He knew that her heart was racing and her entire body felt as though it had been turned into an electric circuit. He knew the effect he was having on her, from the sparks to the quiver in her belly. It was the same effect he had on all women.

'Miss Prince?'

That cold, sardonic voice shocked her out of her stupor.

If she had harboured any hope that he'd forgotten her contribution to his sister's educational experience, then those hopes now lay smashed in tiny pieces at her feet.

'As you know, Polly is the daughter of our chairman and chief executive.' Apparently blind to the unspoken communication, Michael Andrews finally found the courage to speak. 'Her father always made sure she had a job here.'

The implication was that she was some sort of loser who couldn't get employment without help, and Polly felt her temper rise at the injustice of that introduction. The anger was just what she needed to blast away those other feelings.

Relieved to be back in control, she tapped a key on the laptop and opened a file. 'I've prepared a presentation outlining our business strategy and looking at our forecasts for the future. You'll see that we've won six new clients already this year and those accounts are—'

'We don't need to hear this, Polly.' Michael Anderson interrupted her hastily and Polly's fingers paused on the keyboard. Yes, they did. Without her presentation the staff didn't stand a chance of being kept on.

'But you have to—'

'It's too late, Polly.' With a glance at his fellow board members, Michael Anderson cleared his throat. 'I understand that this is a very awkward situation for you, but your father no longer has control of this company. He's always been unconventional, but now he appears to have disappeared completely. Even today, with rumours of the takeover all over the news, there is no sign of him, which just confirms that the board made the right decision to sell. The Doukakis Media Group is cutting edge. These are exciting times.' He cast a fawning glance at the man who sat still and silent at the head of the table. 'There's going to be a shake up. We'll be announcing redundancies to the staff later but I wanted to tell you personally as your father isn't here. It's tough, I know—' he rearranged his drooping features into a look of sympathy '—but this is business.'

Polly felt as though she'd stepped into a parallel universe. Her brain was fuzzy and there was a buzzing in her ears. 'Wait a minute.' Her voice sounded robotic and nothing like her own. 'You're saying you're going to make everyone redundant just like that, with no discussion? It's your job to protect them—to show Mr Doukakis why they're needed.'

'The point is, Polly, they're not needed.'

'I disagree.' Her fingers were suddenly ice-cold. Panic crept into her throat and lodged itself there as if she'd suddenly inhaled all her worst fears. 'The accounts we've won, we've won as a team. And we're a good team.'

'Just leave the laptop, Polly.' Michael Anderson tapped the end of his pen on the table. 'If one of Mr Doukakis's people wants to look at the presentation, they can.'

That was it.

They were dismissing her.

Every eye in the room was fixed on her, waiting for her to give up and walk out.

Her father's company would be dissolved. One hundred people would lose their jobs.

'It isn't over.' The words spilled from her lips and Polly stared directly at Michael Anderson, the man who had sold her father out and was now selling out her colleagues. Desperately, she tried to appeal to his conscience. 'You *have* to stand up there and give this presentation.'

'Polly—'

'You have a responsibility! These people work for you. *They put themselves out for you.* You should be defending them.' The exhaustion and stress of the past week overflowed like a river bursting its banks after heavy rainfall. 'It's because of their hard work that you've been living the high life. Why did you ask me to put together the presentation if you never intended to use it?'

'You were anxious about your father.' Michael's tone was patronising. 'I thought it would keep you busy.'

'I'm not a child, Mr Anderson. I can keep myself busy. I've had no choice about that since the key players in this company do nothing but sit on their backsides eating and drinking their way through the profits.' Dimly aware that she was burning every bridge, she stalked round the table and had the satisfaction of seeing Michael Anderson's eyes widen in consternation.

'What are you doing? Where are you—? I can see you're angry, but—'

'Angry? I'm not angry. I'm *furious*. You have one hundred employees biting their nails out there—' Beyond caring about herself, Polly flung her arm towards the door. 'One hundred people terrified of losing their jobs who right now are wondering whether they're going to be able to afford to keep a roof over their heads and *you're not even going to fight for them?* You're a disgusting coward.'

'That's enough!' His face was red and angry. 'If it weren't for the fact that you're the boss's daughter, you would have been fired long ago. You have a real attitude problem. And as for the way you dress—'

'How a person dresses doesn't affect their ability to do a

job, Mr Anderson. Not that I expect you to understand that. With the exception of the board—' she cast a derisive look around the boardroom table '—this is a young, vibrant, creative agency. I don't need to wear a boring suit with an elastic waistband to accommodate a four-course business lunch paid for by your unsuspecting clients.'

Scarlet-faced, Michael Anderson looked as though he was at high risk of a stroke. 'I'm going to overlook your behaviour because I know how difficult this week has been for you. And I'm going to give you some fatherly advice as your own father seems to take his responsibilities in that area so lightly. Take your redundancy money, go on a good long holiday and rethink your future. Apart from your extremely unfortunate temper, you're a nice girl. Beautiful.' Sweat beading his brow, he dragged his eyes away from her legs. 'You're only working on client accounts because of your father. In any other company you'd be a secretary. Not that there's anything wrong with that,' he said hastily as he saw Polly's expression darken. 'All I'm saying is that a girl with your looks doesn't need to spend her nights with her head in a spreadsheet playing with business—isn't that right, gentleman?'

A murmur of agreement spread through the watching board members. The only person not smiling was Damon Doukakis. He stayed silent, his eyes hooded as he watched the antics from the far end of the table.

Polly saw nothing through the red mist of anger that clouded her vision. 'Don't you *dare* criticize my father. And don't you dare make those sexist, misogynistic comments when we all know who's doing the work in this company. You sold out to the highest bidder for personal gain. You're now multimillionaires and we're unemployed.' She tried and failed to keep the emotion out of her voice. 'Where was your sense of responsibility? Shame on you. Shame on all of you.'

Michael Anderson's mouth was slack with shock. 'Who do you think you are?'

'Someone who cares about the future of this company and the people who work for it. If you make one single one of them redundant before at least considering other options then I'll—' *What?* What could she do? Aware that she was utterly power-less, the anger suddenly left her and Polly turned and stalked back round the table, furious with herself for losing control. She felt spent and exhausted and utterly dispirited. She'd let everyone down. Instead of making things better, she'd made them a thousand times worse.

Damn, damn and damn. Why couldn't she stay cool and calm like these fat, overblown men in suits? Why hadn't she gone to bed last night? Being tired always lowered her burn threshold.

Deafened by the extended silence, Polly felt misery slide through her veins. Her anger had blown itself out, but not before she'd ruined everything. 'Look—I'll go, OK? I'll walk out of here right now without a fuss. Just don't make everyone redundant.' Mortified by her behaviour, she directed her words at Damon Doukakis, who still hadn't made a move. 'Please don't make anyone redundant because of me.' Horrified to feel the hot sting of tears, she closed her laptop and was about to leave the room when Damon Doukakis spoke.

'I want to see that presentation. Send it to my handheld.' His voice hard and inflexible, his eyes locked on Polly with the deadly accuracy of a laser guided missile. 'I want to see everything you've put together.'

Mute with shock, Polly couldn't move, and it was Michael Anderson who recovered first.

'She's just a glorified secretary, Damon. Honestly, you really shouldn't—'

Damon Doukakis ignored him. He was still looking at Polly. 'You can tell the staff they have three months to prove

their worth. The only immediate job losses will be the board.'
That unexpected bombshell sent ripples of consternation
across the room.

As the meaning of his words sank home, Polly felt light-
headed. He wasn't getting rid of the staff. They had a stay of
execution.

Making a strange choking sound, Michael Anderson tried
to loosen the collar of his shirt. 'You can't get rid of the board!
We're the engine of this company.'

'If my car had an engine like you it would have been
scrapped,' Damon said grimly. 'You revealed your commitment to the company when you sold me your shares. I don't
want anyone working for me who can be bought. Nor do I
want to find myself slapped with a lawsuit for sexual discrimi-
nation, which will undoubtedly come my way if you stay with
the company.'

Watching the other man crumble, Polly felt like cheering,
but Damon Doukakis was still speaking, listing his demands
with a complete lack of emotion.

'I'm moving the entire operation into my London offices.
I have two floors empty and a team ready to facilitate the
move.'

Polly's desire to cheer instantly faded. 'But the staff have
been here for ever and—'

'I don't deal in "for ever", Miss Prince. In business, the
best you can hope for is "for now". My second in command,
Carlos, will take over the day to day running of business for
the foreseeable future.'

'But Bill Henson has been in that post for—'

'For far too long,' came the smooth reply. 'He can work
with Carlos for the next three months. If we're impressed,
we'll take him on. I never lose good people. But I run a meri-
tocracy, not a charity.'

Michael Anderson's face was a strange grey colour.

'Damon—' He cleared his throat. 'You need someone to show you our systems. Explain how the company is run.'

'It took me less than five minutes with your balance sheet to assess how the company is run. The word is *badly*. And I've already decided to keep someone on who has inside knowledge.'

Michael sagged and his smile was slack and desperate. 'That's a relief. For a moment there I thought—'

'Which is why Miss Prince will come and work alongside me for the next three months.'

Work alongside him? Oh, no, not that. 'I'm ready to step down, Mr Doukakis.'

'You're not stepping anywhere, Miss Prince. You and your laptop are going to be right by my side as we sort out this mess together.' His words were deliberately ambiguous and Polly wondered which mess he was referring to—the company, or her father's relationship with his sister.

'But—'

'My people will be here within the hour to organise the move into my offices. Anyone who would rather not move is, of course, free to leave.'

'Wait a minute—' Polly felt as if she'd been flattened under a heavy object. She'd assumed she'd be the first out of the door. She was ready and willing to make that sacrifice. In fact she was desperate to put as much distance as possible between her and Damon Doukakis. 'I resign.'

His eyes locked on hers. 'Resign and I'll make the entire workforce redundant this afternoon.' The suppressed anger in him licked through the room, sizzling everyone around the table to a crisp.

'No!' Polly felt dizzy with horror. 'They haven't done anything.'

'Having glanced at your balance sheet, I find it all too easy to believe you. I'm asking myself what anyone in this company has done over the past year. It's only fair to warn you that I don't hold out much hope that these people will still be working for me in three months. I've seen more activity in a graveyard.'

Polly's limbs weakened. She thought about Doris Cooper, who had worked for her father in the post room for forty years. Recently widowed, the woman made a habit of giving the wrong post to the wrong people, but no one wanted to upset her so they quietly reorganised everything when she wasn't looking. Then there was Derek Wills who couldn't spell his name but made lovely cups of tea to keep everyone going. If she walked out they wouldn't even make three weeks, let alone three months. 'Fine,' she croaked. 'I'll work for you. But I think your behaviour is appalling.'

'Your opinion of me is unlikely to be lower than mine of you.' He came right back at her, the full power of his anger slamming into her shaking frame with the force of a hurricane.

Polly stood rigid, impossibly intimidated despite her attempts not to be. There was something terrifying about that splintering dark gaze and the raw power of the man in front of her. She didn't need to see the contempt in his eyes to know he had a low opinion of her and even the heels on her boots didn't help. He still made her feel small in every way possible. But none of that was as scary as the other feelings she was trying so desperately to ignore. *The quickening of her pulse and the strange melting sensation inside her tummy.* 'You're not being fair.'

'Life isn't fair.' His tone was hard and uncompromising. 'Like it or not, you're all now part of my company. Welcome to my world, Miss Prince.'

CHAPTER TWO

HE'D never encountered such a shambolic operation in his life.

Infuriated at having landed himself with a company that offered him no benefit whatsoever, and angrier still at the wanton carelessness the Prince board had demonstrated towards people's job security, Damon cleared the room with a single movement of his hand.

It frustrated him to have to deal with this situation when all he really wanted to do was track down his sister and protect her from the fallout of her own mistakes. Even after an intense week of reflection, he was no closer to understanding what had driven her to make such an appalling decision. Was her choice of Peter Prince just another ploy to prove her independence? Challenge him? He stood for a moment, bracing himself against the crushing weight of responsibility that had been his closest companion since he'd been forced to take charge of his sister's welfare in his teens.

As Polly Prince stalked towards the door with the board members, he intercepted her. Slamming the door shut behind the last suited man, he turned on the woman he hadn't laid eyes on for a decade.

'Wherever you are, trouble is always close behind.'

She was taller than he remembered. Other than that, she didn't seem to have changed much from the rebellious teenager who had stood sullen and defiant in the school office hearing her fate.

Damon scanned her from head to foot in a single sweeping glance, taking her choice of dress to be just another example of her careless, irresponsible attitude to life.

Everyone else had chosen to wear a dark suit to the meeting. It was typical that Polly Prince had favoured fashionable over formal, her short dress revealing incredibly long legs showcased in hot pink tights and black ankle boots. She looked fresh, young and—sexy.

The sudden explosion of primal lust was as unexpected as it was unwelcome and Damon dragged his gaze up from the heels of her cheeky black boots to focus on her face.

Accustomed to mixing with women who dressed with understated elegance, he was exasperated that the self-discipline he exerted over his own responses appeared to have deserted him. Even as he was telling himself that he had more sophistication than to feel sexual attraction for a girl with great legs, he was wrestling with a powerful urge to shrug off his jacket and cover those slender curves.

To kill those unwanted feelings stone-dead, he focused on the issue of his sister and her father. 'Where the hell is he?'

'I don't know.'

'Then tell me what you *do* know.'

Her delicate features were set and determined as she stared directly at him. 'I know you've taken over my father's company. Clearly you're a megalomaniac.' Her cool remark threw petrol onto the fire that raged inside him.

'Don't take me on, Miss Prince. I'm a tough boss but I'm a tougher enemy. Remember that.' He delivered the warning and had the satisfaction of seeing her face lose colour. 'I don't want to hear anything from that smart mouth of yours except answers to my questions. *Where* is your father?'

'I have no idea.'

That unmistakably honest admission was a solid blow to his gut. He'd been relying on her to reveal her father's whereabouts. 'You must be able to make contact. How do you get hold of him in an emergency?'

'I don't.' She sounded genuinely surprised by the question. 'My father taught me to be self-sufficient. If there's an emergency, I handle it.'

'I've taken over your father's company, Miss Prince. This is definitely an emergency and I don't see you handling anything. I can't believe that the CEO of a company can so readily abandon his responsibilities.' It was a lie, of course. He'd seen it before, hadn't he? Tasted first-hand the bitter after-effects of another man's careless disregard for obligation. The memory of it had never left him. Even now, when success was his many times over, it was always there beneath the surface. It drove him forward from one deal to the next. It was the reason he had never relied on another man for employment.

In the midst of discovering that the past still had the power to destabilise him, Damon found his attention snagged by the wisp of pale blonde hair that had floated down from the haphazard, kooky hairstyle she wore. It seemed that even her hair was rebellious.

This girl, he mused, knew nothing about obligation and responsibility.

She selfishly pursued her own agenda with no thought to the casualties. Ten years before it had been his sister who had suffered. Thrusting aside the fleeting thought that Polly Prince couldn't be held accountable for her father's shortcomings, he subjected her to a cold appraisal which she returned with no visible display of nerves or conscience.

'You offered an inflated price for the stock and the board members sold my father out. That was outside my control. My priority now is to do everything I can to protect our loyal staff from your predatory instincts.'

'Cut the act. We both know that you have no interest whatsoever in protecting the staff. The only reason you care about the business is because it's your meal ticket. No other company would be stupid enough to take you on. You've been bleeding this company dry for years, but it's stopping right now. If you were hoping I'd give you a pay-off to leave, then you're in for a shock because I don't carry passengers. You may be the *ex*-boss's daughter, but from now on you're going to work for your money.' The anger boiled up inside him, the past somehow mixing with the present. 'You're going to take your useless, lazy self and finally do a job. And if all you're capable of doing is clean the toilets, then you'll clean the toilets.'

Those sapphire-blue eyes were locked on his and then she made a sound that might have been a laugh. 'You really don't know anything about the company you just bought, do you? Mr Media Mogul who never makes a mistake in business—Mr Big Tycoon who is all-seeing and all-knowing—is suddenly blind.' Her voice dripped contempt and Damon, who prided himself on his lack of emotion in all his dealings, found himself wrestling the temptation to throttle her.

'My only interest in your father's business is as a way of ensuring his co-operation.'

'You have no choice but to be interested in his business. You own it. A fairly heavy-handed approach to a problem, I'd say.'

'I'll do what it takes to protect my sister.' He'd been protecting her since he was fifteen years old—since that cold February night when the policeman had knocked on the door and delivered the shattering news. Losing both parents in such a brutal way had been devastating but Damon had somehow dragged himself through each day, driven by the knowledge that another person was depending on him. He was all Arianna had in the world and what had began as the most terrifying responsibility had become the driving force behind everything he did. Now, protecting Arianna was as natural as breathing. Nothing would destroy the web of protection he'd spun around her. 'If you have any idea where they are, you should tell me now because I will find out.'

'I have no idea. I am not my father's keeper.'

'Arianna is your friend.' He watched with satisfaction as that barb slid home.

'And she's your sister. She's as likely to confide in you as she is in me.'

'She tells me nothing about her life.' The words tasted bitter in his mouth. 'And now I know why. Evidently she has much to hide.'

'Or possibly you're just not an approachable person, Mr Doukakis. Arianna is twenty-four. An adult. If she wanted you to know what she was doing, she'd tell you. Perhaps you should try trusting her.'

Worry fuelled his anger. 'My sister is ridiculously naïve.'

'Had you not been so over-protective, perhaps she would have developed some street sense.'

Damon was thrown once again by the contrast between her fragile appearance and the layer of steel he sensed in her. It had been the same ten years before, when she'd stood in the office in silence, steadfastly refusing to explain her appalling disregard for school rules and general good behaviour. Because of her, his sister had been forced to leave one of the best schools in the country. Damon had subsequently banned Arianna from seeing the appalling Polly Prince. That was before he'd understood how teenage girls worked. The ban had effectively spurred his young sister into full rebellion mode and Arianna had promptly doubled the time she'd spent with the Prince family. It was a decision that had triggered numerous high-octane explosions in the Doukakis household.

'Arianna is a very rich woman. That makes her a target for all sorts of unscrupulous individuals.'

'I don't pretend to be an expert on relationships, Mr

Doukakis, but I do know that my father isn't with Arianna because of her money.'

'Really? Then perhaps you have no idea just how much trouble this company is in.' He wiped his mind of images of his young sister with an ageing playboy.

'Has it crossed your mind that he might be with her because Arianna is warm and funny and my father finds her entertaining?'

The thought of what form that 'entertainment' was likely to take sent pushed his soaring anger levels from dangerous to critical. 'Well, she won't be entertaining him for much longer.' Control slid from his grip. 'How the hell can you be so calm? You should be completely mortified. Your father is—how old?—fifty?'

'He's fifty-four.'

'And it doesn't embarrass you to see his name linked with an endless string of young women? He is thirty years older than Arianna. He's been divorced *four times*. That's a sign of an unstable personality.'

'Or a sign of an eternal optimist, Mr Doukakis.' Her voice was husky. 'My dad continues to believe in love and the institution of marriage.'

If it hadn't been his sister they were talking about, Damon would have laughed. 'The institution of marriage doesn't require endless practice, Miss Prince.' Her defence of her father drove his opinion of her lower still. 'When I walk out of here, I'll be giving a statement to the media. Within the hour news of my takeover will be all over the internet. Once he finds out I have control of the company, your father *will* make contact. When that happens, I want to know. And I want to know immediately.'

'My father doesn't like the internet. He says it inhibits the development of personal relationships.'

At the mention of personal relationships, sweat broke out

under his collar. 'Bad news has a habit of travelling fast and we both know I'm the last person he would want at the helm of his precious company.'

'I agree. He won't be pleased. He considers you to be a man whose only goal is profit. He didn't like me mixing with you when we were teenagers.'

Transfixed by that altogether unexpected revelation, Damon stared at her with genuine astonishment. 'He considered *me* a bad influence?'

'My father has a real thing about people who only judge the world in financial terms. That isn't the way he runs his life and it certainly isn't the way he runs his business. To my father a successful business is as much about the people as the profits.'

'It took me a single glance at your company accounts to work that out. Prince Advertising is afloat through good fortune and the accidental success of a few of your campaigns,' Damon snapped out, noticing that a faint frown appeared on her forehead. 'The company is in profit despite your father's approach to business, not because of it. As for the people— your headcount is severely bloated and you need to slim down. You're carrying dead wood.'

'Don't you dare describe these people as dead wood. Everyone here has an important part to play.' Her voice shook. 'Your fight is with my father, not with the innocent people working for this company. You can't make them redundant. It would be wrong.'

'Business tip number one,' Damon said softly. 'Never let your opponent know what you're thinking. It gives them an advantage.'

Those narrow shoulders straightened. 'You already have the advantage, Mr Doukakis. You've bought my father's company. And I'm not afraid to tell you what I'm thinking. I'm thinking that you're as ruthless and cold as they say you are.' Her eyes shone and he wondered if he should warn her that it was dangerous to wear her emotions so close to the surface. And then he realised how hypocritical that would be because, for once, his own were similarly exposed.

Acting on an impulse he didn't want to examine too closely, Damon reached out and caught her chin in his hand, feeling the softness of her skin under the hard pads of his fingers as he forced her to look at him. 'You're right. I am as ruthless as they say I am. You might want to remember that. And tears just irritate me, Miss Prince.'

'I'm not crying.'

But she was close to crying. He recognised the signs and he could feel the betraying tremble of her jaw. She was the same age as Arianna and yet that was where the similarity ended. For a fleeting moment he wondered what her life must have been like—an only child brought up by her father, a notorious playboy.

'I took nothing your board of directors did not readily give.'

'You made them an offer they couldn't refuse.' Her emotional accusation almost made him smile.

'I'm Greek, not Sicilian. And the people working for me would never sell me out, no matter how good the offer.'

He saw something flicker in her eyes and then she jerked her chin away from his grasp. 'Everyone has their price, Mr Doukakis.'

And she should know, Damon thought grimly, remembering the reason she'd been excluded from school. Definitely nothing like his sister. 'I'm afraid I have to politely decline your offer. When it comes to my bed partners I'm extremely discerning.'

For a moment she stared at him blankly and then her mouth dropped. 'I was talking about business.'

Damon found himself looking at those lips. 'Of course you were.'

'You are *so* offensive. Have you finished?'

'Finished? I haven't even started.' Damon slowly lifted his gaze and stared into her eyes. The chemistry was unmistakable but it didn't worry him in the slightest. When it came to women he made his decisions based on logic, not libido. He had no time for people who were unable to exercise control over their impulses when the need arose. 'At the moment the staff have their jobs. Whether or not they keep them is up to you and your father. I'll expect you in my offices at two o'clock this afternoon. You're going to start doing some work. And don't waste time appealing to my emotions, Miss Prince. I never let emotions cloud my decision-making.'

'Really?' Those blue eyes locked on his and he saw the same fire and determination in her he'd seen that day in the school. 'That's interesting, because I'd say that your decision-making in this instance has been entirely driven by emotion. You're using this takeover as leverage against my father. If that isn't an emotional decision, I don't know what is. And now, if you'll excuse me, I need to organise the staff for the office move. If you really want all this "dead wood" transferred to your offices by this afternoon then I'd better get my useless, lazy self moving.' She stalked towards the door, all long legs and youthful attitude as her dress swung tantalisingly round the tops of her thighs and the spiked heel of her boots tapped the floor.

Hauling his gaze away from the seductive curve of her bottom, Damon slammed the lid on that part of him that wanted to flatten her to the boardroom table and indulge in raw, mindless sex. 'And do something about the way you dress. *Theé mou*, you look like a flamingo in your hot pink tights. I expect the people working for me to look professional.'

'So you don't like what I do and you don't like the way

I look.' Her back to him, she stood frozen to the spot. 'Anything else?'

He wondered if she kept her back to him as a gesture of defiance or because she was close to tears.

There was something disturbing about the fragile set of her narrow shoulders, but Damon was out of sympathy. If she really cared about the staff, the business wouldn't be in the state it was in. Because of this woman and her father Prince Advertising was in a pitiful state and a hundred people now risked losing their jobs. A hundred families risked having their lives shattered. A chill spread down his spine as he contemplated the possible fall-out from that scenario. 'I want all the system passwords handed over to my team so that we can access everything. If I'm going to unravel the mess you've created here I need to know what I'm dealing with. That's it. You can go.'

He could have told her that he considered redundancies a sign of failure. He could have told her that he understood his responsibilities as an employer better than anyone and that he ran his business according to his own rigid principles.

He could have told her all of that, but he didn't.

She'd contributed to this shameful mess.

Let her suffer.

'I'm going to kill him. I'm going to put my hands round that bronzed throat and squeeze until he can't utter another sarcastic word and then I'm going to cut holes in his perfect suit and squirt ketchup on his white shirt...' Feeling powerless, Polly lowered her head onto her hands and thumped her fist on the desk. 'What do women see in him? I cannot *imagine* voluntarily spending a single minute in his company. He's a heartless, sexist monster.' But that hadn't stopped her being hyper-aware of him all the way through their confrontation. There was a sexual energy between them that seriously unsettled her. *How* could she find him attractive?

'I don't know about him being a monster. The man is smoking hot.' Debbie put a stack of empty boxes onto the floor and started clearing the office. 'At least we still have our jobs. Let's face it, the figures are so bad he could have dumped us all and no one could really have blamed him.'

Knowing that it was true, Polly lifted her head and stared at her friend in despair. 'Trust me, that might have been the better option.'

'You don't mean that.'

'I don't know what I mean, but I know I can't work for that man.' Exhausted and stressed, she tried to blot out images of his cold, handsome face. *Cold*, she reminded herself. *Cold, with no sense of humour.* 'I'm not going to last a week. The only thing in doubt is whether I kill him before he kills me.'

'You can't walk out! The future of the staff depends on you staying!'

'How do you know that?'

'We were listening at the door.'

Polly sank down in her chair. 'Have you no shame?'

'This was a crisis. We needed to know whether to ring the job centre or not.'

'Ring them anyway. You won't want to work for him for long.' Trying to galvanise herself into action, Polly tugged open the drawer in her desk and stared down at the jumble of belongings. 'I need a different pair of tights. Hot pink clearly isn't his favourite colour. I cannot *believe* I'm about to change my clothes because a man asked me to. How low can a girl go? I should have told him where to stuff his dress code but I'd already antagonised him more than I should have done.'

'He didn't like the tights?' Debbie raised her eyebrows. 'Did you tell him you're wearing them because—?'

'*Tell him?*' Polly rummaged through the drawer. 'No one

tells Damon Doukakis anything. They just listen while he commands. This is a dictatorship, not a democracy. How the hell does the man keep his staff?'

'He pays top rate and he looks bloody gorgeous.' Debbie stacked books into the boxes. 'Calm down. I know you're angry, but look on the bright side—he fired the board. And you were *brilliant.*'

'I lost my temper with Michael the Moron.'

'I know. You were amazing. You really let him have it. Pow. Smack.' Debbie abandoned the packing and punched the air like a boxer. 'Take that you sexist pig. No more looking up our skirts. No more demanding cups of coffee while we're all running round like demented baboons doing the work he's too lazy to do. We were all cheering.'

'There's nothing to cheer about. Haven't you ever heard the phrase out of the frying pan into the fire? Damon Doukakis is a macho control freak with serious anger issues—' Polly silenced the internal voice that reminded her that he was protecting his sister. That was no excuse to go completely over the top.

'You can forgive a man a lot when he looks like that.'

'I'm not interested in the way he looks.'

'Well, you should be. You're young and available. I know you're anti-marriage because of your dad, but Damon Doukakis scores a full ten on the sexometer.'

'Debbie!'

'Oh, chill, will you? You've been uptight all week. It's bad for your blood pressure.'

Polly had her nose back in the drawer. 'I don't have any boring black tights.'

'Just wear leggings. Here's a box—start packing.'

She took the box and forced herself to breathe slowly. Even though she'd grown up knowing that sex and love were two different things, the sexual tension between her and Damon horrified her. 'I wouldn't touch the man with a long pole. Apart from the fact that I can't be attracted to a man who doesn't smile, I wouldn't want to have sex with a guy who is about to make a load of innocent people redundant. It doesn't show a caring personality.'

'You can't expect him to smile when he's taking over a company as unusual as ours.' Debbie closed the box she was packing and started on another. 'Most people just don't get the way we work here. I mean, I love it, but we're not exactly conventional, are we? Nothing about your dad is conventional.'

'Don't remind me.'

'Relax. When your dad finally emerges from wherever he is this time, at least he'll still have an intact company even if it does belong to someone else. If Demon Damon was thinking of making everyone redundant immediately he wouldn't be mobilising an army of removal people to transport us from economy city to Doukakis World.' Debbie carefully lifted a plant. 'I'm excited. I've always wanted to see inside that building. Apparently there's a fountain in the foyer. The plants are going to love that. So are the fish. Running water is very soothing. He must care about his employees to give them something as lovely as a fountain.'

'It's probably there so that despairing employees can drown themselves on their way out of the building.' Polly walked across to the noticeboard she had on her wall and started taking down photographs.

'You always say that everyone has a sensitive side.'

'Well, I was wrong. Damon Doukakis is steel-plated. There's more sensitivity in an armoured tank.'

'He's super-successful.'

Polly stared at a photograph of her father standing on a table at a Christmas party with a drink in one hand and a busty blonde from Accounts in the other. 'Whose side are you on?'

'Actually, Pol, I'm on the side of the person who pays my salary. Sorry if that makes me an employment slut, but that's the way it has to be when you have dependants. Principles are all very well, but you can't eat them and I have two cats to feed. Careful with those photographs.' Debbie looked over Polly's shoulder and gave a nostalgic sigh. 'That was a good night. Mr Foster had one too many. He's been nice to me ever since that party.'

'He's a lovely man but he's not a very good accountant. He won't last five minutes if Damon Doukakis decides to analyse what he does.' Overwhelmed with the responsibility, Polly carefully slid the photographs into an envelope. 'I'm sure the Doukakis financial department are killer-sharp, like the boss. They're not going to be impressed when they see Mr Foster using a pen and a calculator. It will destroy him to lose his job.'

'Maybe he won't. You've been teaching him to use a spreadsheet.'

'Yes, but it's slow going. Every morning I have to go back over what we did the day before. I was hoping we could sneak him past the inquisition without anyone actually wanting to know what he does but it isn't going to be easy. I bet Doukakis knows if his staff stop to draw breath.' The responsibility swamped her. 'Debs, we can't give him a reason to let anyone go. Everyone has to pull their weight and if they can't pull their weight then we have to cover for them.'

'So this probably isn't a good time to tell you that Kim's child-minder is sick. She's brought the baby into the office because that's what she always does, but...' Debbie's voice tailed off. 'I'm guessing Damon doesn't have a soft spot for babies.'

Swamped by the volume of work facing her, Polly tipped the contents of a drawer into the box without bothering to sort it. 'Tell Kim to quietly take the rest of the day working from home, but get her to try and find childcare for tomorrow.'

'And if she can't?'

'We'll give her an office and she can hide in there. I suppose it's a waste of time asking if my father has phoned? I'm going to fit him with an electronic tagging device. Did you phone any of those hotels I gave you?'

'All of them. Nothing.'

'I wouldn't put it past him to have bribed some blonde hotel manager to keep his booking quiet.' Polly put the photographs into a box. 'We need to get the rest of this packed up. The barbarian hoards from Doukakis Media Group are going to be descending on us any minute to help us move.'

'The takeover is headlines on the BBC. You dad must know by now.'

Polly paused to swallow two painkillers with a glass of water. 'I don't think he's exactly watching television, Debs.'

'Do you have any idea who he's with this time?'

Yes.

Her father was with Arianna, a girl young enough to be his daughter.

Humiliation crawled up her spine as she anticipated the predictable reaction from everyone around her. Polly was no more eager to share the information with the world than Damon Doukakis.

For once in his life, couldn't her father have picked someone closer to his own age?

'I try not to think about my father's love-life.' Dodging the question, she crammed the lid onto the box. 'I just don't see how we can move our entire office in the space of a few hours. I'm exhausted. All I want to do is go to bed and catch up on sleep.'

'So go to bed. You know how chilled your dad is about

flexitime. He always says if the staff don't want to be there, there's no point in them being there.'

'Unfortunately Damon Doukakis is about as chilled as the Amazon jungle. And he wants me in his office at two o'clock.'

Debbie's eyes widened. 'What for?'

'He wants me to start working for my money.'

Debbie stared at her for a moment and then burst out laughing. 'Sorry, but that's *so* funny. Did you tell him the truth?'

'What's the point? He'd never believe me and he's made it his personal mission in life to make my life hell.' Polly ripped off a piece of tape and slammed her foot down on the bulging box to flatten the lid. 'So far he's succeeding beyond his wildest fantasies.'

Debbie picked up a stack of prospectuses from universities. 'What do you want me to do with these?'

Polly stared at them and felt slightly strange. 'Just shred them.' If Damon Doukakis found those on her desk, he'd laugh at her. 'Get rid of them. I should never have sent off for them in the first place.'

'But you've always said that what you want more than anything is to—'

'I said, shred them.' She resisted the impulse to grab them and stow them carefully in a box. *What was the point?* 'It was just a stupid dream.'

A really crazy dream.

Numb, she watched as her hopes and dreams were shredded alongside the paper.

Five hours later, exhausted from having supervised the packing of the entire building and seen the staff safely into the coaches laid on to transfer them to their new offices, Polly took her first step into the plush foyer of the Doukakis Tower. The centrepiece was the much talked about water feature, a bubbling monument to corporate success, blending seamlessly with acres of glass and marble. Blinded by architectural perfection, Polly could see why the building was one of London's most talked about landmarks.

Directed to the fortieth floor by the stunning blonde on the futuristic curved reception desk, she walked towards the glass-fronted express elevator. From behind her she heard the bright-voiced receptionist answer the phone. 'DMG Corporate, Freya speaking, how may I help you?'

You can't, Polly thought gloomily. *No one can help me now. I'm doomed.*

Everywhere she looked there was evidence of the Doukakis success story.

Used to staring at a crumbling factory wall from her tiny office window, she felt her jaw drop in amazement as she saw the view from the elevator.

Through the glass she could see the River Thames curving in a ribbon through London and to her right the famous circle of London Eye with the Houses of Parliament in the distance. It was essentially a huge glass viewing capsule, as stunning and contemporary as the rest of the building. Damon Doukakis might be ruthless, she thought faintly, but he had exceptional taste.

Depressed by the contrast between his achievements and their comparative failure, Polly turned away from the view and tried not to think what it would be like to work for a company as progressive as this one. Everyone employed by him probably had a business degree, she thought enviously.

No wonder he'd been less than impressed with her.

She stared at herself in one of the two mirrored panels that bordered the doors of the elevator and wondered how she could prove to him that she knew what she was doing.

She was now working for the most notoriously demanding boss in the city of London. She still wasn't really sure why he'd kept her on instead of just firing her along with the board. Presumably because he saw her as his only possible link with her father.

Or possibly just to torture her.

Once the shock of seeing the board of directors leave the building had faded, the staff had erupted into whoops of joy, relieved to still have their jobs. Surprisingly, even the thought of moving to new offices didn't seem to disturb people. Everyone seemed excited about the prospect of a move to more exciting surroundings.

The only person not celebrating was Polly.

She didn't know much about Damon Doukakis, but she knew that he didn't do anyone favours. He was keeping people on for a reason, not out of kindness. When it suited him to let them go, he'd let them go. Unless she could persuade him that the staff were worth keeping.

All morning she'd multitasked, talking to clients via her wireless headset while packing up boxes and masterminding the move. Somewhere in the middle of the chaos she'd stripped off her pink tights and replaced them with black leggings. It was her one and only concession to the strict Doukakis dress code.

Now, she wondered if she should have avoided conflict altogether and worn a suit. Trying to summon sufficient energy to get through the rest of the day, she slapped her cheeks to produce some colour and ignored the hideous squirming in her stomach.

First days, she thought grimly. *She hated first days.* It was like being back at school. Whispers behind her back. *Is that her?* The humiliation of her father driving her to school in a flashy car with his latest embarrassingly young wife installed in the front seat. Giggles heard across the length of a playground. Mysterious collisions in the corridor that sent her books flying and her self-esteem plummeting. Standing alone in the lunch queue and then finding an empty table and trying to look as though eating alone was a choice, not a sentence.

Polly glared at her reflection in the mirror. If those days had taught her anything it was how to survive. No matter what happened, she was not going to let Damon Doukakis close down the company. Not without a fight.

Somehow, she had to impress him.

Wondering how on earth you impressed a man like Damon Doukakis, she pressed the button for the executive floor and the doors of the elevator slid closed. But at the last minute a gloved male hand clamped itself around the door and they opened again.

Her hope for two minutes peace dashed, Polly squashed herself back against the far corner as a man dressed in motor-bike leathers strode into the lift. She caught a glimpse of wide, powerful shoulders and realised that it was Damon Doukakis himself.

Their eyes clashed and she had a sudden urge to bolt from the lift and use the stairs.

The temperature in the tiny capsule suddenly shot up.

He didn't even have to open his mouth, she thought desperately. Even the way he stood was intimidating. Irritated by the fact that he looked as good in leather as he did in fine wool, Polly raised an eyebrow.

'I thought we were supposed to wear suits?'

'I had a meeting across town. I used the motorbike.' He wore his masculinity like a banner, overt and unapologetic, and Polly was horrified to feel her insides liquefy.

'So you don't change into leather just to beat your staff.'

The glance he sent in her direction was both a threat and a warning. 'When I start beating my staff,' he said silkily, 'you'll be the first to know because you'll be right at the top of my list. Perhaps if you'd had some discipline at fourteen you wouldn't have turned out to be such a disaster. Evidently your father didn't ever learn to say no to you.'

Polly didn't tell him that her father had abdicated parental responsibility right from the beginning. 'He had trouble handling me.'

'Well, I won't have trouble.' His tone lethally soft, he took in her appearance in a single glance. 'I'll give you marks for being on time and for changing out of those fluorescent tights.'

For some reason she couldn't fathom, his derision brought a lump to her throat. She had blisters on her hands from carrying boxes that were too heavy, her feet ached, her back ached, and she hadn't slept in her bed for four nights. And just to add to her frustration her phone had stopped ringing. All morning clients had called her, but now, when she was desperate for a senior client to ring her for advice so that she could sound impressive and prove to Damon just how good she was at her job, it remained silent.

And there was no point in telling him, was there? He'd made up his mind about her based on that episode in her teens and the state of her father's company.

The whole situation was made a thousand times worse by the fact that a small part of her knew she was deserving of his contempt. It *was* because of her that Arianna had been excluded from school. It didn't surprise her that he had such a low opinion of her. What surprised her was how much she cared. It shouldn't matter what he thought of her. All that mattered now were the jobs of the innocent people who worked for her father.

'The headlines on the one o'clock news were pretty brutal. They're calling you the hatchet man.'

'Good. Perhaps it will bring your father out of hiding.' His sensuous mouth curved into a grim smile as he hit a button on the panel and sent the lift gliding upwards.

Transfixed by his mouth, Polly felt her stomach drop. His features were boldly masculine, from the hard lines of his bone structure to the subtle shadow that darkened his jaw. Desperate, she looked for evidence of weakness but found none. 'My father isn't hiding.'

'Miss Prince—' his voice was a soft, dangerous purr '—unless you want to experience first-hand experience of the impact of my temper in an enclosed space, I suggest you don't force me to think about what your father might currently be doing.'

Polly instinctively retreated against the glass. 'I'm just saying he isn't hiding, that's all. My father isn't a coward.' London slowly grew smaller and smaller until it lay beneath them like a miniature toy town. By contrast, the tension in the capsule rocketed.

'He's allowed his business to decline rather than make the difficult decisions that should have been made. He needed to make serious cuts but he chose not to do it. If that isn't cowardice, I don't know what is.'

'You shouldn't make judgements on something you know nothing about.'

'I run a multinational corporation. I make difficult decisions every day of my life.' His innate superiority infuriated her almost as much as the fact that he was right. Her father *should* have made some difficult decisions. But the fact that it was Damon Doukakis who was now pointing that out somehow made it more difficult to hear.

'I'm sure it gives you a real feeling of power to fire people.'

It happened so fast she didn't see him move, but one moment she was standing with an aerial view of London and the next she was staring at wide shoulders and a pair of fiercely angry eyes. 'Never before have I had to restrain myself around a woman, but with you—' He drew in a shaky breath, clearly struggling with the intensity of his own emotions. 'You are enough to provoke a saint. Trust me when I say you do *not* want a demonstration of my power.'

Polly stared at him in appalled fascination, wondering why everyone thought he was Mr Cool. He was the most volatile man she'd met. He simmered like a pan of water kept permanently on the boil. *And he smelt incredible...* 'I was just making the point that you really work this whole I'm-the-boss-and-you're-going-to-do-it-my-way routine.' *Please let him step away from her before she gave into the temptation to bury her face in his neck and just breathe.* 'We're used to a more relaxed approach when we work. Frankly I'm not sure how well we'll do under a reign of terror.'

Outrage rippled across his shoulders and his jaw clenched. 'That *relaxed approach* has sent your company plunging towards bankruptcy. If any redundancies come from this disaster then you and your father will be responsible.'

Brain-dead with exhaustion, Polly felt a perverse sense of satisfaction at seeing him so angry. She wanted him to suffer too. Not just for giving her the most hellish week of her life, but also because she had a desperate urge to crush her mouth to his and feeling that way aggravated her in the extreme. 'You're obviously not enjoying having us as part of your business,' she said sweetly. 'Next time perhaps you should check out your prey before you swallow it. We're obviously giving you indigestion.'

He released her as suddenly as he'd trapped her, stepping back with an exclamation in Greek that she was sure wasn't complimentary.

'The press have somehow guessed that your father and my sister are together.' Lifting a hand, he yanked down the zip of his jacket as if it were strangling him. 'Unless you enjoy fuelling gossip, I suggest you don't talk to them. I've instructed my people to put out a statement on the takeover, concentrating on our corporate vision and goals. I'm trying to focus attention on the fact that your company fits logically within my current business.'

'You mean you don't want to admit publicly you're a megalomaniac who bought a company just so that you could threaten the man having a relationship with your sister.' But she was horrified by the news that the press now had the story. She knew it wouldn't be long before they were digging for reasons and she didn't even want to think about what that would mean. She'd been there before and she loathed it. Everyone wanting to know how it felt to have a stepmother the same age as her. Everyone appalled and fascinated by the ridiculous antics of her father.

'Take a tip from me, Miss Prince.' Those thick dark lashes descended until the look in his eyes was virtually obscured 'even in this age of sexual equality, no real man wants to spend time with a bitch or a ball breaker. Try and cultivate a softer, more feminine side and who knows? You might find yourself a boyfriend. Possibly even one who owns a company that you can play in.'

Polly was so shocked she couldn't speak. She didn't know what appalled her most. The fact that he had this entrenched image of her as a lazy waste of space, the fact that he'd clearly asked someone about her sex-life, or the fact that part of her was wondering how he kissed.

Putting it down to tiredness, she promised herself a *really* early night. 'I'd never be interested in a man who couldn't cope with a strong woman.'

'There's strong and then there's strident, which is presumably why you're still single.'

Only the knowledge that she'd be confirming his less than flattering assessment of her prevented her from launching herself at him. Instead she smarted furiously and kept her eyes fixed on the streets shrinking beneath their feet. *This is good*, she told herself. *If he keeps this up all I'm going to want to do to him is kill him and that feels better than sizzling chemistry.* 'If the doors opened to the outside, I'd push you.'

His laugh lacked humour. 'If I thought we'd be working together for long, I'd jump.'

Boiling inside, Polly was saved from thinking up a response by the muted 'ping' of the doors as they glided silently apart, revealing a cavernous, light-filled office space.

Damon propelled her forward and she stepped into an open-plan office area like nothing she'd ever seen before.

Taken aback, momentarily forgetting their heated exchange, she stopped walking and just stared.

Despite everything she'd heard and read about Damon Doukakis, nothing had prepared her for the bustling efficiency of the Doukakis corporate headquarters. 'Oh…' She looked at the bank of desks, each with a video phone, a laptop plug-in and a printer. Most were occupied and there was no questioning the industry of those working. Barely anyone looked up from what they were doing. 'Where—?' Puzzled, she turned her head and looked around her at the clean, unclut-tered workspace. 'Where's their stuff? Where do they keep books, magazines, family pictures—personal things. It's all very Spartan.'

'We operate a hot desk system.'

Her mind preoccupied, Polly suddenly had an image of everyone burning themselves when they sat down to work. 'Hot desk?'

'Employees don't have their own fixed office space. They come in and sit at whichever work station is free. Office space is our most expensive asset and most offices only use fifty percent of their capacity at any one time. We lease the lower ten floors of this building. It's a highly profitable way of maxi-mising the space.'

'So people don't actually have their own desks? That's

awful.' Genuinely appalled, Polly tried to envisage her friends and colleagues existing in such a sterile environment. 'But what if someone wants to put up a photograph of their baby or something?'

'When they're at work they should be working. They can stare at the real live baby on their own time.' Damon Doukakis urged her through the floor, occasionally pausing to exchange a word with someone.

Polly examined the faces of the people, wondering what it must be like working in such soulless surroundings. Granted, you could have sold tickets to look at the view from the windows, but nothing about the office space was cosy. 'There's nothing personal anywhere.'

'People are here to do a job. They have everything they need to do that job. People who work for me are adaptable. Technology allows for workforce mobility. Commuting is time-consuming and expensive. I'd rather my people worked an extra two hours than spent those hours sitting in traffic. Some people work flexible hours—start late, finish late. They'll be sitting down at a desk when another person is leaving it. If they're out of the country for a meeting, then the desk is used by someone else. This is the office template of the future.'

Except that Damon Doukakis had brought the future into the present.

Polly thought about the office she'd just left. Until they'd been forced to strip it bare, the walls had been covered in framed copies of their advertising campaigns, photographs and pictures of past office parties. On her desk she'd kept numerous objects that cheered her up and made her smile. And she had Romeo and Juliet.

Here, there were no walls on which to put photographs. No cosy staffroom with soft armchairs and a gurgling coffee machine. Everywhere she looked there was chrome, glass and an industrious silence.

Hoping fish weren't afraid of heights, she stared around her. 'So is this going to be our floor?'

'No. I'm showing you an example of efficiency in action. Take a good look around, Miss Prince. *This* is how a successful company looks. To you it probably feels like landing on an alien planet.' His sensuous mouth curved into a sardonic smile. 'In order to cause minimum disruption to the rest of my operation I've allocated a separate floor to your operation.' Without waiting for her response, he pushed open a door and took the stairs two at a time. Polly poked her tongue out at his back and followed more slowly, envying his athleticism.

Following him through another set of doors, she found herself on another floor, completely circled in glass.

All the boxes and equipment had already been transferred from her old offices and the staff of Prince Advertising were laughing and joking together as they unpacked.

As they waved to her, Polly felt her eyes sting. They were so optimistic and excited. They had no idea how fragile their future was.

The responsibility almost flattened her.

'This is yours.' Damon gestured across the floor with his hand. 'There are meeting rooms over there, all of which can be used for sensitive phone calls that can't be made in open plan.' As he finished speaking the lift doors opened and Polly saw Debbie and Jen stagger out of the lift carrying boxes. After a series of 'oohs' and 'ahhs' as they saw the view, they put down the boxes.

'This is the last of it. Now we can start settling in. Won't take us long to make the place home. Not that my home looks anything like this,' Debbie said cheerfully. 'Where's the kettle?'

Polly caught sight of the shock in Damon Doukakis's eyes

and realised that the only way she was going to stand a chance of preserving jobs was if she kept everyone as far away from the boss as possible. She had to protect them. 'Mr Doukakis, I haven't had a chance to send that presentation through to you. I copied it onto a flash drive so you can open it up on your own computer. Debs, if you could supervise the unpacking, that would be great.'

'Sure thing. I'll have to work out which of the plants like sunlight because there's a lot of sunlight in this building.' Deb tugged off her shoes and prepared to get stuck into the work. 'This place is epic.'

'Whatever you need to do.' Deciding that the reason the staff appeared to have no internal radar warning them of danger was because they'd worked for her father for so long, Polly frantically tried to distract their new boss. 'Perhaps we should have the meeting in your office as there is going to be some disruption on this floor.'

'Disruption appears to be a comfortable working environment for you. Are those—' he did a double take as Debbie reached into another box and, together with Jen, lifted out a huge bucket '—*fish*?'

Oh, God.....

'You gave us four hours' notice of an office move,' Polly muttered. 'There wasn't time to negotiate relocation. We'll have the tank set up in no time and no one is even going to know they're here.'

'Tank?!'

'You're the one who insisted the whole company move here. The fish are part of the company.'

'You keep fish?'

'Look at it this way. They're not going to bother anyone and you don't have to pay them. They're motivational without being costly.'

Her feeble attempt to lighten the situation fell flat. Damon

Doukakis didn't smile. Instead he turned his gaze on Polly. Silence spread across the room and Polly was hideously aware that everyone was listening.

The atmosphere changed from one of carnival to one of consternation.

Pinned by that intense, dark stare Polly felt his disapproval slam into her with lethal force.

'My office,' he growled. 'Right now.'

CHAPTER THREE

'TAKE my calls, Janey.' Dropping his phone onto his PA's desk, Damon strode into his office with Polly following close behind.

The moment he heard the door close, he turned, intending to launch a blistering attack on the sloppy, unprofessional attitude of her staff, but the sight of her swaying in the centre of his enormous office killed the words before they left his mouth.

He'd never seen anyone more miserable or more exhausted.

Whatever else was going on, he could see Polly Prince had had one hell of a week. It couldn't have been easy watching her cushy life slip through her fingers. A few more strands of that shiny blonde hair had escaped from the restraining clip on top of her head, there were black smudges under her violet eyes, and her cheeks were the same pristine white as his shirt.

Standing in the centre of his enormous office, she reminded him of a lone gazelle that had lost the rest of its herd.

'What?' She was watching him warily. 'Do you think you could stop frowning at everyone? It's really hard to operate in an atmosphere of terror.'

'I do *not* create an atmosphere of terror.'

'How do you know? You're not the one on the receiving end.'

'We do three-hundred-and-sixty-degree reviews here. If staff feel *afraid*, they have the opportunity to say so.'

'Unless they're too afraid to say so.' Tiredness laced itself through her voice and suddenly her shoulders drooped slightly, as if the effort of maintaining all that attitude was just too much. 'Look, I know you think I'm a complete waste of space and actually...' She paused and pushed her hair away from her face. 'Actually, I don't completely blame you for that because all the evidence points in that direction, but sometimes things aren't entirely as they seem.'

'Your company is a circus. What exactly isn't as it seems?'

'We may look chaotic to you, but we work well in a relax, informal atmosphere. It helps us be creative.'

'If that's your way of asking if you can keep the fish, the answer is no. I don't allow pets in my offices.'

'Romeo and Juliet aren't pets, exactly. They're an integral part of the workforce. They cheer people up and staff motivation is hugely important. I'm asking you to relax your rigid principles for five minutes. You might be surprised what a bit of work enjoyment does.'

'What I think,' Damon said slowly, 'is that the way you do business is sloppy and unprofessional.' And the irony was, he wasn't even interested in the business. He'd taken control in a desperate attempt to flush Peter Prince out of hiding but so far it hadn't worked. There had been no contact.

The knowledge that Analisa could have called him and hadn't added layers of pain and anxiety to his anger. She always accused him of being over-protective, and maybe he was, but was it really being over-protective to want to prevent someone you loved from being hurt?

The affair was doomed, and the thought of having to deal with a heartbroken Arianna sent a cold chill through his body.

Once before he'd held her as she'd sobbed and he never wanted to do that again. *Never wanted to see his sister that sad.*

Polly was frowning at him. 'Look, I know this whole thing

is a mess, but give me a chance.' There was a desperate note to her voice. 'Now that you've got rid of the board, I know I can turn this company around.'

'*You?*' Her astonishing claim momentarily distracted him from thoughts of his sister.

'Yes, me. At least let me try.'

For the first time since he'd walked into the Prince headquarters, Damon felt like laughing. 'You're asking me to give you free rein to do more of what you've been doing?'

'I know you won't believe me but I *do* know what our business needs to make it successful.'

'It needs someone at the helm who isn't afraid to take tough decisions. The fish have to go. I'm not running an aquarium. All you need to do your job is a laptop and an internet connection. I assume you have heard of both those things?'

But he had to admit he was surprised by her vigorous and ongoing defence of the staff. She appeared to care passionately whether they lost their jobs or not.

Presumably it had finally come home to her that if the company crashed, she'd be out of a job and an inheritance.

So pale she looked as though she might pass out, she walked towards him and put a flash drive on his desk. 'The file you want is on there. Look at the numbers. Ninety percent of our expenses were attributed to one percent of the staff. You just got rid of that one percent. Those same people were on the highest salaries but made the smallest contribution to the company. You just made a massive saving on our operating costs.'

Damon found himself distracted by the tempting curve of her lower lip. 'I'm surprised you even know what an operating cost is.'

'Please open the file.'

Ruthlessly deleting thoughts of sex, Damon slid the flash

drive into his computer and opened the document. 'Do I read from the beginning of this fairy story?'

'It isn't a fairy story. You'll see from this that we've pitched for six new pieces of business in the last three months. We won all six accounts. One of those was against your own advertising team. We beat them. The client said our pitch was the most creative and exciting he'd seen.' There was an energy and confidence about her that was at odds with his impression of her and Damon was genuinely surprised.

'Creative and exciting doesn't send a company bankrupt.'

'No, but high overheads can. And so can bad management. We suffered from both.'

'Your father was in charge. Who exactly are you blaming?'

'Blame is a waste of time. I'm just asking you to look at the facts and help us move forward.' She hesitated. 'I know you're good at what you do, but we're good too. Together we could be incredible. I'll be downstairs helping the staff settle in if you want to talk about this. Start by looking at these figures.' She leaned across his desk and pressed a key on his computer and a strand of that rebellious hair floated against his cheek, soft as down.

Damon lifted a hand to brush it away at the same time she did and her fingers tangled with his. Scarlet-faced, she jumped back, clearly as horrified by the contact as he was.

'You don't need my help with this—just—it's self-explanatory.' She tucked the offending strand behind her ear and Damon watched, transfixed by those delicate fingers tipped with painted nails.

'Is that—?' His attention caught, he narrowed his eyes and squinted at her nails but she quickly whipped her hands behind her back.

'Just take a look at that presentation.'

'Show me your hands.'

There was a mutinous flash in her eyes but she stuck out her hands. 'There.'

'You have a skull and crossbones painted on your nails.'

'It's called nail art. I use different stencils.'

'And you chose a skull and crossbones for today?'

She gave a tiny shrug. 'It seemed appropriate. Look, I know you think this is all frivolous but one of our clients owns a major brand in nail colour. We did a fantastic cover mount on one of the big women's glossies last summer, and— Never mind—it's all in the figures. What are you doing?' The stream of nervous chatter died as he took her hands firmly in his.

Making a sound in her throat, she gave a little pull but Damon tightened his grip. Her hands were smooth and delicate and he was blinded by a sudden image of those slim fingers closing around a certain part of him.

Raw sexual awareness burned through his body, brutal in its intensity. He felt her hands tremble in his. The confidence and assurance melted away from her, leaving confusion in its place.

Damon wondered if the air-conditioning in his office had broken. The atmosphere had suddenly become heavy and oppressive.

Even as he was in the process of reminding himself that this girl's father was the source of his current problems, she snatched her hands away and stepped back. 'I'll leave you to read the presentation.'

Damon felt mildly disorientated.

What the hell was he doing?

'Yes. Go.' If she hadn't already been leaving of her own free will he would have ejected her from his office with supersonic speed. Not wanting to examine his own behaviour too closely, he dragged his gaze back to the document on the screen but all he saw was golden hair and long nails.

Forcing himself to focus, he concentrated on the first slide.

One glance told him that it had been prepared by someone computer literate and numerate. In fact it was the first sign of professionalism he'd seen since he walked through the doors of Prince Advertising.

He stopped thinking about Analisa and analysed the data in front of him.

'Wait—' He stopped her as she reached the door. 'Who did this?' His rough demand was met by a long, pulsing silence and then she turned to face him.

'I did.'

'You mean Mr Anderson gave you the information and you collated it.'

'No, I mean I put together the information I thought you'd need to be able to make an informed decision about the future of the company.'

Damon glanced at the complexity of the data on the screen and then back at her. 'I consider it a serious offence to take credit for someone else's work.'

A wry smile tilted the corners of her mouth. 'Really? It makes a refreshing change to hear that from someone in authority. Maybe we'll work well together after all.'

Damon stared at the spreadsheet, trying to make sense of what he was seeing. 'What exactly was your official role in the company?'

'I was my father's executive assistant, which basically means I did a bit of everything.'

A bit of everything. 'So this isn't Mr Anderson's spreadsheet?'

'Mr Anderson couldn't switch the laptop on, let alone create a spreadsheet.'

Damon leaned back in his chair. 'So you're good with computers?'

'I'm good with a lot of things, Mr Doukakis. Just because I wear pink tights and have fun with my nails it doesn't make me stupid any more than wearing jeans would make you approachable.' She still had her hand on the door handle, as if she was ready to run at a moment's notice. 'I need to get back downstairs. Having your future in someone else's hands is very traumatic for everyone. It would mean a lot if next time you go down there you could maybe smile or say an encouraging word.'

'They should be grateful I've taken control. Without me your business would have been bankrupt within three months.' And in an attempt to protect his sister he'd landed himself with still more responsibility for jobs and lives. He felt like Atlas, holding the heavens on his shoulders.

'We've had problems with our cash flow, but—'

'Is there any part of the business you *haven't* had problems with?'

'The clients love us because we're very creative.' She looked him in the eye. 'All I want is your assurance that there will be no redundancies.'

'I can't make that assurance until I've unravelled the mess your father has created.'

'I *know* parts of the business have problems. I'm not going to pretend they don't. But I'm asking you to look deeper and learn about how we work before you make an irrational decision.'

'Irrational?' Brows raised with incredulity, Damon leaned forwards in his chair. 'You think I make irrational decisions?'

'Normally, no. But in this case—' she breathed slowly '—yes. I think you're so angry with my father, and you feel so helpless about your sister, you were willing to do anything that might give you back some element of control. And as for the way you feel about me—you haven't forgotten I'm the reason your sister was permanently excluded from school at fourteen. I really messed that up, I admit it, but don't use something *I* did ten years ago to punish the staff. That wouldn't be fair.'

Damon sat still, forced to acknowledge that there was at least a partial truth in her accusation. Had he been unfair to judge her on something that had happened when she was still young? 'Go and settle the staff in downstairs.' His tone was rougher than he'd intended. 'I'll call you if I have any questions.'

An hour later he had more questions than he had answers. Exasperated, he hit a button on his phone and summoned his finance director. 'Ellen, can you come in here?' His eyes still fixed on his computer screen, he drummed his fingers impatiently on the desk. 'And bring the salary details for the Prince people. There's something wrong with the numbers.'

Moments later he was staring at another set of figures that still didn't make sense. Trying to unravel the puzzle, he stood up abruptly. 'According to this information, all of these people took a salary cut six months ago. And his daughter has barely been paid a living wage for the past two years.'

'I know. I've been going over the figures too.' Ellen spread the summary pages over his desk. 'The company is barely afloat. It's a small agency with the overheads of a big agency.'

'But the board are primarily responsible for those overheads.' Polly Prince had been right in her assessment, he thought grimly. The board had been sucking the company dry. First-class flights. Elaborate lunches. Thousand-pound bottles of vintage wine….. The list went on and on.

'They're in serious financial trouble. They've been hit by the economic downturn but made no compensatory moves. Peter Prince badly needed to trim staff. Instead they appear to have agreed to take a cut rather than allow anyone to be laid off.' Ellen adjusted her glasses. 'The business is a mess of course, but you knew that when you bought it. On the plus side they have some surprisingly good accounts and somehow they've just won a major piece of business with the French company Santenne. Their leading brand is High Kick Hosiery. That's going to be huge. Didn't our people pitch for that?'

'Yes.' The news that they'd lost out to Prince Advertising did nothing to improve Damon's mood. 'So how did Prince win it? They're the most shambolic operation I've ever encountered.'

'That's true. Financially and structurally they're a disaster. Creatively—well, I assume you've seen this?' A strange light in her eyes, his finance director handed him a folder she'd brought with her.

'I haven't seen anything.'

'But you always research companies so carefully.'

'Well this time I didn't.' His tone was irritable and Ellen looked at him calmly.

'We've worked together a long time, Damon. Do you want to talk about this?'

'No.' Damon shook his head and lifted a hand. *'Don't* ask.'

'I'm guessing this has something to do with your sister.' Her tone was sympathetic. 'She's lucky to have you looking out for her.'

'I wish she felt the same way.'

'That's because she takes your love for granted. Which is a compliment. It means she feels secure. Trust me, I know. I have teenagers. You've done a good job.'

It didn't feel that way, but the prospect of discussing it horrified him almost as much as the situation itself. 'About this company—'

'It's not all bad news.' Fortunately Ellen took the hint and changed the subject. 'There is a creative brain at work there. You just need to harness it.'

Damon opened the file and slowly flicked through the pages. Pausing, he lifted a glossy advert featuring a teenager in a nightclub. 'That's clever.'

'It's all clever. And creative. The customer profiling is spot on. Their use of social networking is astonishingly astute. My eldest has been nagging me to buy this for months, all based on the pester power generated by their campaign.'

His interest piqued, Damon flicked through rest of the folio. 'The creative thinking is original.' He frowned down at the tagline under a famous brand of running shoes. '*"Run, breathe, live."* It's good.' Staring at the work, he remembered Polly's words.

'Clients love us. We're very creative.'

'Their sales have quadrupled since that campaign went live. They tapped into the whole lifestyle thing. There is no doubt that Prince Advertising is a mess, but there's at least one person in the company who is exceptional. I'd go as far as to say they're afloat purely because of the talents of their creative director. Who is he?'

'His name was Michael Anderson and I fired him.' Damon was staring down at the pages in front of him. 'And there's no way these ideas came from him. The man didn't have an original thought in his head.'

'Maybe it was Prince himself?'

Just thinking of Peter Prince sent Damon's tension levels shooting skyward. 'He's in his fifties and he's notorious for abandoning the company when it suits him. From what I can gather he treats it more as a hobby than a business. This stuff is young. Fresh. Visionary.'

Ellen smiled. 'And fun.'

Fun.

Damon thought of the skull and crossbones on Polly's nails. The hot pink tights. The fish on the desk. The party atmosphere that hit him every time he went near the staff. 'They certainly have an interesting work ethic.'

'So if it wasn't the creative director, who's coming up with the ideas?' Ellen gathered up the papers. 'Thanks to their creativity they have some major pieces of business. Their billing is haphazard, their cash flow is a nightmare, but we can sort that—' she shrugged '—and absorb them into our business. Just make sure we don't lose the brain behind these campaigns. We need to find out who it is and lock them into a watertight contract. Any idea who it could be?'

'No.' Mentally scrolling through the people he'd met, Damon closed the file. 'But I intend to find out immediately. And I know just the person to ask.'

By seven o'clock Polly was the only one left on her floor of the office. She'd spent the latter half of the day juggling problems and soothing frayed nerves while taking endless calls from anxious clients who had seen news of the takeover on the TV.

'Mr Peters, I think we should be reviewing the whole media mix.' Sitting cross-legged on the floor, she talked into her headset so that her hands were free to unpack the last of the boxes, 'Yes, it's true that Mr Anderson has gone.' She retrieved a packet of balloons from the bottom of the box and slid them into her desk. 'But there are other people more than qualified to advise you on the best strategy.' *Like me*, she thought, rescuing the charger for her BlackBerry and adding it to the stuff accumulating in the drawer. 'I'm going to schedule a meeting in your diary, get the team to put together some ideas and then we'll present them to you. I promise you will be blown away by our ideas… Uhuh…mmm, definitely…absolutely top priority.'

When she finally hung up, she keyed in the task to the ever-growing to-do list in her BlackBerry and carried on sorting out her desk area. The rest of the staff had gone home hours before, all apparently excited by the prospect of riding down to street level in the glass elevator.

Left alone, Polly removed her boots and settled down to an

evening of hard work. Darkness spread slowly over the city as she worked her way steadily through her calls. After a few hours she glanced up at the towering panes of glass and saw that the view had changed from daytime city-slick to night-time sparkle and she paused for a moment, captivated by the wide-angled view of London at night. The moon sent a sliver of light across the River Thames and for the first time in a horrid, hideous week she felt peaceful.

Maybe, just maybe, this could turn out to be a good thing. Damon Doukakis was probably one of the few people with the talent to turn the company round, providing he didn't fire all of them first.

Romeo and Juliet seemed happy enough in their new sur-roundings and Polly had discovered that there were enough workstations for everyone without having to operate the Doukakis 'hot desk' system. She wondered how his employ-ees must feel, coming to work every day and sitting down at an empty, featureless surface, greeted by nothing more than a power point and a phone socket.

Damon Doukakis was focused on the success of his busi-ness to the exclusion of everything else.

She paused in the middle of deleting an e-mail.

Well, not *quite* everything else.

Her cheeks burned and she stared down at her hands, re-membering. The attraction had been like a searing blade, driven straight through her. And she was pretty sure he'd felt it too.

He'd looked horrified, she remembered, which should have dented her ego except that she was a realist. There was no way he would sully himself with a mongrel like her. She'd seen enough pictures of him in the gossip columns to know that the women he chose were sleek and groomed. Elegant. Dignified. Controlled. Everything about his life was ruthlessly controlled, from work to women.

Polly looked down at herself. The women he dated would no more dream of sitting shoeless and cross-legged on the floor unpacking a box than they would be seen in public without perfectly blow-dried hair.

Wondering why she was wasting time thinking about what sort of women Damon Doukakis dated, Polly finished emptying the box and put it ready for recycling.

Her desk was covered in pink sticky notes with various phone messages taken by Debbie while she'd been on the phone to other people.

Urgent. Call Vernon White about the Honey Hair campaign.

Ring the media buyer at Cool Campaigns about the media strategy for Fresh Mouth mints.

David Mills from Fox Consumer wants to talk urgently...

Urgent, urgent, urgent. It was all urgent. She felt a rush of panic as she contemplated all the work she still had to do. Everyone had heard the news of the takeover and was wondering whether Prince Advertising was going to exist in a month. And she couldn't give them an answer. She had no idea what Damon Doukakis intended to do so all she could do was sound positive and up-beat.

Knowing that if all her clients walked in the opposite direction then the staff would definitely lose their jobs, Polly peeled off the notes one by one and added the calls to the list. Then she settled back into her cross-legged position on the floor and worked out a priority for the morning.

She was wondering whether it would be any help to get a second phone, when she heard the swish of a door opening and saw Damon Doukakis striding towards her.

Her confidence melted away like chocolate held in a child's palm.

When it came to work she was more than ready to fight her corner but she had no idea how to fight these other feelings that squirmed inside her whenever she was in the same room as him.

Once glance at the exquisitely cut black dinner jacket and bowtie told her that his plans for the evening were infinitely more exciting than hers and she held her breath as he approached. His startling good-looks made it impossible to do anything but stare when he was in the room. It didn't help that he carried himself with that inborn confidence that seemed genetically embedded in people born into wealth. It had been years since she'd felt that awful creeping sense of inferiority but she felt it now as she stood trapped by those glittering dark eyes.

Polly's head began to spin and suddenly she was glad she was sitting down, because at least sitting down didn't require strength in one's legs. It was just the tiredness, she told herself. Nothing more. He wasn't *that* gorgeous.

As he stood looking down at her from his formidable height, she was forced to revise that opinion. OK, so maybe he was gorgeous. To look at. But it was all on the surface.

Feeling out of her depth, she made a vague attempt to defuse the crackling tension. 'Nice outfit. I didn't know you had a second job as a waiter.'

There was no answering smile and she felt a flash of relief. There was no way she could ever find a man without a sense of humour remotely attractive, even if he *did* have an incredible body that did miracles for a dinner jacket. She told herself that the flutter of nerves in her stomach was down to the ominous look in his eyes as he scanned her appearance.

'*Theé mou*, why are you sitting on the floor? Where are your boots?'

'Under the desk. I was emptying boxes and my heels kept catching in my hem—' Realising that his eyes were fixed on her legs, she felt her body heat. 'Never mind. I promise to wear shoes when I see a client, so save the lecture.'

'You have absolutely no—' He broke off in mid-sentence, his attention snagged by the dramatic transformation of his previously ordered office space. '*What* happened here?'

'You told us we could do what we wanted with the space.' Knowing that she sounded defensive, Polly scrambled up from the floor, acutely conscious of his height now that she wasn't wearing her heels. She followed his appalled gaze and saw the calendar of half-naked firemen someone had stuck to one of the steel rods that supported the ceiling. *Oops.* 'That was a project we did for one of our clients. It's a photographic masterpiece, don't you think? We put it up because it helps us to think creatively.'

A dark brow lifted in mockery. 'The more I discover about your creative process, the more fascinated I am.'

Polly shrugged awkwardly. 'I accept we're a bit more— er—informal than you, but to be honest the whole "hot desk" thing doesn't really work for us. I think we're very possibly cold desk people. Or maybe lukewarm desk. We like knowing where we're going to sit instead of playing musical chairs when we come to work every day. We like having a *home*. A little space to call our own.'

'The place looks like a Sunday market.' He picked up the pink fluffy pen she always kept on her desk, his gaze incredulous. 'What do you do with this thing?'

'I write with it. If I'm brainstorming ideas I need to doodle on paper. It helps me think.' Exhausted, her head throbbing, Polly wished she'd hidden the pen. 'It's my happy pen. I like it. It makes me smile and I'm more creative when I'm happy.'

'Well, that's good, because obviously your happiness is my first priority.' His silky-smooth tone held a deadly edge. 'Talking of happiness, how are the fish settling in? Are they homesick? Enjoying the view? Anything I can get them to make them feel more comfortable?'

She decided to ignore the sarcasm. 'Just don't get too close. They're afraid of sharks.'

'I am *not* a shark, Miss Prince.'

'You just gobbled up my father's company in one mouthful so forgive me if I disagree with you.'

'We both know I have no interest in your father's business.'

'Which is a shame, because you're stuck with us now.' Suddenly she appreciated the irony of it. 'You're stuck with our pink, fluffy, fish-loving approach to business and we're stuck with your empty-desk-eyes-forward-don't-anybody-laugh ethos. Interesting times ahead.'

Suddenly, Polly was too tired to fight and she surreptitiously slid her pink notebook under a file in the hope that it wouldn't draw his attention. 'Can I please have my pen back? It's a lucky pen. All my best creative ideas have come while I'm holding it.'

The bold curve of his brows came together in a frown and she wondered what she'd said this time. He obviously thought she was a complete numbskull. 'Could you stop frowning? It's so unsettling. We're used to working in a positive atmosphere.'

He studied her for a long moment and then dropped the pen back on her desk. 'Have you heard from your father?'

'No.'

'Doesn't the man ever call you?'

With that single sentence he unwittingly dug a knife into the most vulnerable part of her. Afraid he might see the hurt, Polly kept her eyes down. 'We live independent lives.' And not for anything would she betray how much this latest episode was upsetting her. She wasn't going to give Damon Doukakis the satisfaction of knowing she was as miserable about the whole thing as he was. 'Was that all? Because I'm pretty busy.'

There was a brief silence and then he surprised her. 'You look exhausted. You need to stop for the day.'

The fact that he'd noticed sent a flicker of warmth through her body and that feeling frightened her more than the power he wielded. The last thing she needed was to think of him as sympathetic. 'I can't stop for the day. My boss thinks I'm a lazy slacker and I have another million phone calls to make before I go home.'

'You can't go home.' He picked up a stuffed bear she kept on her desk and studied it with an air of baffled incredulity. 'There is a mob of journalists outside just waiting for one of us to leave so that they can bombard us with questions.'

Polly snatched the bear out of his hands. 'I'm not scared of journalists.'

'I'm not talking about a few intrusive questions.' He was still looking at the bear as if he couldn't quite believe what he was seeing. 'I'm talking about a horde of people hungry for juicy scandal. You and the stuffed bear can stay in the apartment tonight.' He reached into his inside jacket pocket and withdrew a plastic card. 'Take the lift up to the top floor. This opens the door. The security is more sophisticated than the Bank of England. You'll be safe there.'

He was offering her sanctuary from the press?

The unexpected gesture destabilised her. Staying in the apartment would mean she could carry on working and clear some of the backload. 'Well, that's—if you're—thanks,' she said gruffly. 'How do you plan to avoid them?'

'My car is in the underground car park.' He glanced at his watch. 'I have to go, but tomorrow we're going to talk about that presentation of yours. I have questions.'

'Right. But I can't talk tomorrow. I'm going to Paris for a client meeting.'

'What time is your flight?'

'I'm not flying, I'm catching the train. It leaves at seven-thirty. The meeting is in the evening.' Realising how that sounded, she coloured. 'They moved the meeting after I booked my train.'

'And you thought you'd have a day in Paris.' The brief moment of harmony had been blown away and contempt was stamped on his hard, handsome face.

His continued censure was too much for her after a long and stressful day and she glared at him defensively. 'It was an economy ticket. I couldn't move it.'

'I've seen the company expense account.'

'No, you've seen the *directors'* expense account.'

'Who are you meeting in Paris?'

'Gérard Bonnel, the Vice President of Marketing for Santenne. He was there when we pitched for the business. Now he wants to go over our ideas.'

'You cannot meet someone of Gérard's seniority on your own. I'll come with you. And for God's sake wear a suit before you come face to face with a client.'

Polly opened her mouth to argue but he was already striding across the floor towards the elevator.

Her confidence well and truly punctured, she stared after him and decided that she'd rather stab herself in the eye than sleep in his apartment. So what if a few journalists were waiting for her outside? She'd dealt with journalists before. And she was so tired and moody they'd probably take one look at her face and realise the danger of getting too close.

Exhausted and dejected, Polly worked for another hour and then pushed her feet into her boots, dropped her phone into her pocket and enjoyed the silent, panoramic downward glide in the elevator. The thought of Damon Doukakis joining her on her trip to Paris horrified her. She just wanted to get on with her work and avoid him as much as possible.

She was just wondering whether there was some way she

could lose him at the train station when the lift doors opened onto the foyer.

Glancing towards the security guard who was occupied with a group of people at the desk, she stepped out onto the street and was instantly mobbed.

'*Polly, do you have a statement about Damon Doukakis taking over your father's company?*'

'*Have you heard from him?*'

'*Is there any truth in the rumour that he's with Damon's sister?*'

An elbow lanced her kidneys and Polly winced and turned. 'Ow! Just mind where you—' Jostled and pushed, she lost her balance and her head smashed against something hard and cold. There was a blinding flash and something hot and wet trickled down her face.

Blood, she thought dizzily, and then the world went black.

CHAPTER FOUR

'SHE *what*? Which hospital?' Abandoning his date in the middle of dinner, Damon pocketed his phone and strode out to the limo, his security team clearing the throng of journalists who haunted his every move. 'How badly is she hurt?'

'The hospital wouldn't give details, sir.' Franco, his driver, manoeuvred skilfully through the heavy London traffic. 'Just told me it was a head injury, but they're keeping her in overnight so it must be bad.'

Undoing his bow tie with a few flicks of his fingers, Damon leaned back against the seat of the car and attempted to rein in his frustration.

Why the hell had she left the building? He'd left precise instructions that she should stay in the apartment. Instructions she'd apparently ignored.

The girl was an utter disaster.

Part of him was tempted to leave her to suffer for her own stupidity but another part was acutely aware that she was on her own in hospital and no one knew how to contact her father.

A thought suddenly occurred to him. 'Ring the press anonymously, Franco. Make sure they know she's in hospital.'

His driver glanced in the rearview mirror. 'They put her there, boss.'

'I don't mean the tabloids, I mean broadcast media. Ring the news desk. Tell them that Miss Prince has been badly injured in an accident and we don't know how long she'll be in hospital. Keep it vague and worrying. I want the story on the next news headlines. With pictures, to make sure they know which hospital.'

Surely hearing news that his only daughter was in hospital should flush Peter Prince out from hiding?

Optimistic that this latest development could be turned to his advantage, Damon forced himself to relax as they negotiated traffic but his underlying concern for his sister was growing with every hour she failed to make contact.

Arianna had been six years old when their parents had died. Landed with the towering responsibility of caring for her, Damon had grown up overnight. He'd understood that she was now his responsibility. That it was his job to prevent his little sister from being hurt. What he hadn't realised it was that the biggest threat to her happiness would come from Arianna herself.

What if she did something stupid like marrying the guy?

Fifteen minutes later his limousine pulled up in the ambulance bay of the large city hospital and Damon sprang from the car and strode into the emergency department, relieved to be able to focus on something other than the dubious life choices made by his sister.

The hospital was heaving but the crowd of people at the desk took one look at him and parted like the Red Sea.

The receptionist immediately sat up straight and smoothed her hair. 'Can I help you?'

'I'm looking for a friend of mine.' Damon bestowed his most winning smile on the dazzled woman. 'Polly Prince. She was knocked out and brought in by ambulance. I expect she's on a trolley somewhere.'

'Prince—Prince—' Her expression glazed, the girl finally dragged her eyes from his face and checked the records. 'Cubicle One. But you can't—'

'Is that left or right?' Well aware of the effect he had on

women, Damon wasn't afraid to use it to his advantage when it suited him. 'I'm so grateful for your help.'

'Left through the double doors,' she said breathlessly. 'The doctor is with her.'

'*Efaristo*. Thank you.' Flashing her a smile, he strode through the doors before anyone had time to challenge him and found himself in a cubicle, empty except for a doctor who looked as though she were about to explode.

Damon felt a flash of empathy. 'Don't tell me. You just had an encounter with Polly and now you need to go to anger management classes.' In one glance he took in the empty trolley and the bloodstained bandage. 'Where *is* she?'

'She just discharged herself against medical advice. We wanted to admit her for twenty-four hours observation but she says she can't possibly stay because she has things she has to do. She's certainly a strong minded young woman.'

Damon thought back to that day at the school when Polly had stuck out her chin and resolutely refused to explain her outrageous behaviour to anyone. Strong-minded was a polite description. 'Why did she discharge herself?'

'She said she had too much to do, but what she should be doing is lying down and resting. She's had a nasty bang on the head.' Clearly annoyed, the doctor slipped her stethoscope back into her pocket. 'She mentioned a trip to Paris and a meeting with an important client. We couldn't get her to let go of her phone. It was welded to her hand right the way through my examination.' The doctor relented. 'I have to admit her dedication impressed me.'

Struggling to reconcile the word 'dedication' with Polly, Damon wondered if he and the doctor were talking about the same person. 'So you're saying that you advised her to stay in, but she walked out?'

'That's right. She'll probably be all right at home as long as she isn't on her own. Just make sure you know what to look out for and you can bring her back in if anything about her condition unsettles you.'

Damon didn't waste time correcting the doctor's assumption that he'd be spending the night with Polly. Instead he scanned the exits. 'Which way did she go?'

'She went out of the ambulance entrance. She said she had a lift home.' Puzzled, the doctor looked at him. 'I assumed that was why you were here?'

But Damon was already on his way out of the door, his phone in his hand as he instructed his driver to bring the car round. 'Have you seen Polly Prince?'

'No.'

Damon swore fluently and then looked around him. Even this late in the evening the hospital was buzzing with activity. There was no sign of Polly. 'Which is the nearest underground station?'

'I believe it's Monument, boss.'

Following a hunch, Damon slid into the car. 'Let's go. Take the most obvious pedestrian route.'

Within two minutes he saw her, walking with her head down and her shoulders hunched, looking as though she were going to collapse at any minute.

'Pull over.' Damon sprang from the car and was next to her in three strides. '*Theé mou*, do you have a death wish? First you leave the office when I warn you about the mob, and then you discharge yourself from hospital against doctor's orders. *What is wrong with you?* Why do you have this urge to do the opposite of what you're told?'

'Damon?' Bemused, she turned her head and he saw the bloody streaks in her blonde hair and the purple shadow darkening one side of her face.

'*Maledizione.* They *hit* you?'

Looking distinctly disorientated, she glanced from him to

the limousine and then back again. 'What are you doing here? I thought you were on a date.'

'I was told you'd had an accident.'

'But what is that to do with you?'

'Naturally I immediately went to the hospital.'

'Why "naturally"? Why would you even care that I was in hospital? You're not my next of kin.'

Frustrated that she would question what had been a natural decision to him, Damon raked his hand through his hair. 'Your father is absent and clearly you couldn't be left to cope with something like that alone.'

'I deal with things on my own all the time. And, frankly, from the way you've been speaking to me all day I was under the distinct impression that given half a chance you'd put me in the hospital yourself. Are you telling me that you abandoned your date because you heard I was hurt?'

'I didn't "abandon" her,' Damon breathed. 'I arranged for her to be driven home.'

'But you deprived her of the pleasure of your company and the promise of bedroom athletics. Wow.' Her mouth tilted into a crooked smile. 'Poor her.'

Ignoring her flippant tone, Damon lifted a hand and touched the side of her head. 'What the hell happened?'

'They jostled me and I lost my balance and fell into a camera. It had hard edges. But I'm fine. It was kind of you to check on me, but I can get myself home.' She tried to dodge past him and he caught her arms in tight grip. Her body brushed against his and the subtle scent of her perfume wound itself around his senses.

He gritted his teeth, wondering why control was such an effort when he was with her. 'You cannot travel on the underground and you're not supposed to be sleeping alone tonight.'

'Are you volunteering to sleep with me?' She gave an

awkward laugh. 'I wish you could see your face. Relax. I know you'd rather cuddle up with a bed bug than have me in your sheets.'

Damon, who had a disturbingly clear idea of what he'd do to her if she were in his sheets, ignored that comment. 'Why did you discharge yourself?'

'I have to go to Paris tomorrow and I still have some ideas to finish off.'

'*Obviously* you won't now be going to Paris in the morning.' Damon drew her towards him as a group of passers-by jostled them.

'Yes, I will.'

'If your father were here, he'd stop you going.'

She didn't look at him. 'No, he wouldn't. I make my own decisions about what I do, and I'm going to Paris.' Twisting herself out of his grip, she turned and carried on walking towards the underground station.

Never having encountered anyone quite as stubborn as Polly, Damon stood for a moment, his emotions veering between exasperation and concern. Clearly she wasn't prepared to listen to reason so what was he supposed to do? Fling her over his shoulder?

Noticing two men staring hard at her legs, Damon decided that wasn't a bad idea. In four strides he caught up with her. 'Why is it so important that you get to Paris tomorrow? Are you sleeping with the client or something?'

A choked sound came from her throat and she stopped dead. 'You really do have a high opinion of me, don't you?'

Heat crawled up the back of his neck. 'I know Gérard. Like most Frenchmen, he appreciates a beautiful woman. And you *are* arriving nine hours before your meeting.'

'Which naturally means I'm leaving plenty of time for afternoon sex before we move from bedroom to boardroom, is that it?' Ignoring the flow of people around them, she fixed those blue eyes on him. 'Make up your mind. This morning you told me I looked like a flamingo and now you think I've turned into a *femme fatale*? Or does a bruised head suddenly make you feel all protective and macho or something?'

He wasn't sure what he was feeling and Damon certainly didn't need her to question behaviour that he was already questioning himself. 'I'm just asking myself what makes this meeting so important that you'd discharge yourself from hospital against medical advice.'

'Everybody's jobs are under threat. He's a new client and I work in the service industry!' Hauling her bag more firmly onto her shoulder, she glared at a man who brushed past her. 'And before you make another insensitive remark, not *that* sort of service industry.' She turned away again but this time Damon shot out a hand and halted her escape.

'You are intentionally misunderstanding everything I say to you.'

'There is another interpretation for the phrase "you look like a flamingo"?'

'I was commenting on the inappropriateness of your dress. I never said you weren't beautiful.' The words launched themselves from some unidentified part of his brain and his own shock mirrored the confusion he saw in her eyes. He released her immediately, disconcerted by the lethal sexual charge that seemed to power every contact, no matter how small. 'Look—you can't be on your own tonight and any minute now the press waiting in the hospital will realised you've legged it out of the back door. Get in the car before you're mobbed for a second time.'

'I don't need a lift. And I have to go back to my house to get my things for the meeting tomorrow.'

'I'm *trying* to help you.'

'And I'm trying to tell you that I don't need help. I handle things myself. I always have.'

'Well, tonight I'm handling them.' Damon held out his hand. 'Give me your keys. Franco will drop us and then go on to your house to get whatever it is you need. You can make him a list in the car. I'll decide if you're well enough to go to Paris in the morning. Until then you'll stay in the penthouse. If you'd done that the first time you wouldn't be in this mess now.'

There was a stunned silence and then she gave a strangled laugh. 'Do you always take control?'

'When the situation demands it, yes.'

'So you're inviting me to stay at your place?' Her eyes glinted a beautiful sapphire blue. 'Aren't you afraid I'll throw a wild party? Sully the place with my wanton ways? You know me—I can't resist any opportunity to indulge in men and alcohol.'

He ignored her reference to the incident at school. 'Hopefully a bang on the head will quell your intrinsic desire to cause havoc. I'll take the risk.' Even as he said the words, part of him was wondering what the hell he was doing creating a situation where they'd be in close contact.

'I appreciate the gesture, but I'm fine. I'm used to looking out for myself.' She added that last observation in a gruff little voice that made him wonder exactly what role her father had played in her life.

Damon was about to probe further when he caught movement out of the corner of his eye. 'We have company. Let's move.'

With that, Damon scooped her up and deposited her in the back seat of the limo, slamming the door shut just seconds before the press pack descended. 'Drive.'

Polly had conflicting emotions as she stepped out of the car in the underground car park of the Doukakis Tower. Smarting at being literally dumped in the car, but relieved at having escaped the hungry press pack, she eyed the high security steel doors that had closed behind them. 'The place is like a fortress.'

'It can be a fortress when it needs to be.' Without looking at her, Damon strode towards the elevator, his footsteps echoing on the concrete.

Polly followed more slowly, and not just because her whole body was starting to ache from her fall.

What was the matter with him now?

It was obvious that he was angry but she had no idea why.

Having locked her safely in the car, he'd proceeded to converse in Greek with his driver, leaving her to stare out of the tinted glass and stew in her own emotions.

'Are you angry because I ruined your evening or because I don't slavishly follow orders? Because I didn't *ask* you to come to my rescue. I would have been fine.'

'Which bit would have been fine, exactly?' He strode into the elevator like a man on a mission and thumped his palm against the button. 'The bit where you were knocked unconscious or the part where you discharged yourself from hospital against medical advice?'

'I'm capable of making my own decisions.'

He looked unimpressed. 'Anyone can make a decision. The skill is making the right one at the right time.'

'That's what I do.'

'What you do, Miss Prince, is disagree with me on principle.'

'That isn't true.'

'Isn't it? You were about to be mobbed by journalists for a second time in one evening. Would you have got into the car if I hadn't forced you?'

She shifted uncomfortably, suddenly realising just how

much she'd inconvenienced him. 'Yes, I would. If you'd given me time to think about it.'

'We didn't have time to debate options.' His savage tone intensified her growing guilt.

'I'm sorry! I loused up your evening and I feel bad about that. And I'm grateful to you for helping me out. I'm not just not—well, I'm not used to accepting help. It feels strange.' Polly felt as small as a field mouse. Not only had he come to her rescue, he'd abandoned a hot date to come to the hospital and all she'd done was give him grief.

When had anyone ever come to her rescue before?

When had anyone given her any help?

A strange, unfamiliar feeling spread through her and she wondered whether the bang on the head had been worse than she'd thought. Suddenly she was relieved he'd forced her into the car. It felt as though a heavy metal rock group was rehearsing inside her skull and she was wondering whether discharging herself had been such a clever idea. Was it normal to feel this bad?

But she had to get to Paris, didn't she? Winning the High Kick Hosiery account was crucial to the business. And they couldn't afford to lose that business.

'P?' Polly focused her gritty, tired eyes on the glowing panel as the lift moved upwards. 'P for prison? P for punishment?'

'Penthouse.'

'Of course. Penthouse. You live above the shop.' Looking at him, she saw how tightly he held onto control and wondered what it took to make him snap. 'I really am sorry I ruined your evening.' Gingerly, she touched her fingers to her head. 'I didn't realise they'd be that eager for a story. How did you find out?'

'My head of security rang me. He was close enough to see

it happen, but not close enough to stop it. Why didn't you stay at the hospital?'

'I can't stay in hospital. I have a very unsympathetic boss. He told me to take my lazy, useless self and do a proper day's work.'

'So I'm to blame for your decisions?'

'Well those were your words but no, you're not to blame. I would have done the same thing regardless of what you said. The meeting is important.' The movement of the elevator was starting to make her feel sick. 'It's tough out there. If I don't deliver, Gérard will just pick up the phone to the next agency on his list. I don't want that to happen.'

'I am *not* an unsympathetic boss.' He spoke the words through gritted teeth. 'And anyone with any sense would take time off after an injury like that. Or are you trying to impress me?'

'I'm not stupid enough to think I could ever impress you.' She wondered why being trapped in a confined space with him should make it hard to breathe. 'I'm just trying to get the job done. The meeting tomorrow is important. With everything so unstable, I can't not turn up. We worked hard to win that business and we need to show them that we can do a good job. Do you have any painkillers in your fancy apartment?'

He breathed deeply. 'Yes.' Even with his top button undone and his bow tie dangling round his neck, he looked sleek and handsome. He also looked supremely irritated.

Polly wondered about the woman he'd abandoned halfway through a date. Who was she? Someone exceptionally beautiful, obviously, who wouldn't dream of wearing hot pink tights or writing with a fluffy pink pen.

She stole a glance at his profile.

No one had ever come to her rescue before. Even the time she'd come off the trampoline at school and broken her arm she'd had to get a taxi home from the hospital because no one had been able to contact her father. Confused by her own feelings, Polly looked away quickly. She was so used to rescuing herself that it felt strange having someone else step in. Thanking someone for help was a whole new experience. 'You could go back and spend the rest of your evening with whoever she is. It isn't too late. I don't need a babysitter. I'm just going to have a bath, wash off the blood—that sort of thing. Go and finish your date.'

'Since you seem determined to launch yourself from one disaster to another, you need supervision.'

Polly laughed and then wished she hadn't because the movement amplified the pain in her head. Supervision? She hadn't been supervised since she was a toddler. Right from the moment she could walk, her father had expected her to sort her own problems out.

Find a way, Pol.

'Unless you're planning on lying down on the bed next to me, I don't see how you can supervise me.' As his eyes met hers, she wished she hadn't used those words. It was uncomfortably easy to think about sex around this man and she wasn't used to thinking about sex. 'I'm going to be fine. I just need painkillers and sleep, that's all. I don't need company for that.'

But the comfort she felt at knowing he was going to be close by shook her. Why did it matter? She'd never been a dependent sort of person. Just because the man had broad shoulders, it didn't mean she had to lean on him.

Seriously unnerved, Polly was relieved when the elevator doors finally slid open and she could put some space between them.

Like everyone, she'd heard whispers and speculation about the duplex apartment that graced the top of the building. Everyone had. When the Doukakis Tower had been under construction there had been hushed talk of the penthouse with its three-hundred-and-sixty-degree views of London, roof garden and glass enclosed heated swimming pool. None of the rumours had prepared her for reality.

'Oh—' Stunned into silence, she stared at the sparkling cityscape that stretched in every direction. The architect had created a space to maximise the view and yet had managed to merge contemporary with homely by dividing that space into distinct living areas.

Polly had never seen so much glass in one place. 'Well—no one is ever going to suffer from claustrophobia here,' she said faintly. 'It's amazing. Seriously cool.'

'I like the feeling of space. My villa in Greece is modern. I like light.'

It was the first personal thing he'd said to her and Polly stood awkwardly, realising just how useless she was at making small talk with men. 'You have a villa in Greece? Lucky you.' *God, what a lame response.* No wonder he thought she was a complete idiot. He was obviously regretting playing nursemaid instead of continuing his date with someone who was no doubt a master at sophisticated conversation.

Chewing her lip, she decided to pretend he was a client. She never felt tongue-tied or awkward talking to clients, did she?

Damon gestured to the end of the room where the space narrowed. 'You can use the guest suite at the end of this floor. I'll show you where.'

Polly took one look at the thick white rugs covering the polished wooden floor and automatically tugged off her boots. Padding after him, she felt like a stray dog that had wandered into someone's home. 'It really is incredible.' Gazing longingly at the deep, luxurious sofas, she followed him through the apartment. Despite the glass and the space it was surprisingly cosy and she felt a stab of envy. This man didn't lie awake at night worrying about how to keep his company afloat and protect people's jobs. He was so phenomenally successful his only worry about money would be how to count it all.

She caught a glimpse of a futuristic-looking kitchen and he intercepted her look.

'Are you hungry? I can ask my chef to make you something.'

'Not unless he does pasta with painkiller sauce. Honestly, I couldn't eat. But thanks for the thought.' For the first time Polly noticed the spiral staircase rising from the centre of the room. Cleverly lit by tiny spotlights, it looked like something from a fairy tale. She'd never considered herself remotely romantic, but suddenly she was wondering if he'd ever carried a woman up that transparent staircase the way he'd carried her to the car…

'Polly?' His rough tone cut through her daydream. Scarlet-faced, she followed him through to a large guest suite and caught her breath. Flames flickered in a sleek, contemporary fireplace and the bed was positioned to take advantage of the spectacular view. It was as if someone had twisted a million fairy lights around every building in London.

Any guest staying here would never want to leave, she thought wistfully.

'The bathroom is through that door. You have blood in your hair—' He lifted a hand and then lowered it again as if he was unsure whether to touch her or not.

The relentless pull of sexual awareness was like an invisible rope dragging them together.

With a faint frown he took a step backwards and they both started to talk at the same time.

'I don't expect—'

'Do you want help?'

No one had ever asked her if she wanted help before and it threw her—but nowhere near as much as the sudden urge to say yes. It was only the thought of stripping off in front of him that kept her from accepting his offer. 'I'll be fine now. I appreciate you bothering.' Part of her wished he hadn't. By helping her he'd tipped the balance of emotion. To feel angry with him was ungrateful, but to feel grateful was uncomfortable. It felt strange, she realised, to know that someone was looking out for her, even if only because of a sense of duty. It turned out that his advice not to leave the building had been sound and when he'd heard she'd got herself in trouble he'd come straight to help her.

Maybe he was ruthless, but he was also decent.

And horribly, terrifyingly attractive.

Damon reached forward and pressed a button by the bed. The cuff of his shirt shifted, the movement revealing a strong wrist dusted with dark hairs. A television screen appeared in the wall but Polly didn't notice. She was transfixed by the contrast between white silk and bronzed male skin.

She swallowed hard. This was worse than she'd thought.

She was in a seriously bad way if she found a man's wrist sexy.

'I'm expecting news of your accident to hit the headlines within the hour. If your father is watching, then he's going to get in touch. If he tries to contact you I want you to dial two on the phone by the bed. It goes through to the master suite.'

Her mind was so busy creating an image of what he would look like naked that it took Polly a moment to process what he was saying. News of her accident? 'There weren't any TV cameras there. They were just photographers and a couple of reporters. It's not going to be on the news.'

'Yes, it is.'

His words sank slowly through her bruised skull. 'But—you *told* them?' Images of him naked vanished in an instant. It was as if someone had pulled the power cord on her brain. Sickness rose inside her and her cheeks flamed as she acknowledged her own gullibility. 'Oh, my God—you used my accident as a publicity stunt.'

'I was not responsible for your accident. *You* made the decision to leave the building and take on a pack of gossip-hungry journalists.' His cool response was the final straw.

Reeling from the discovery that his help had been driven by a desire to flush her father out of hiding, Polly grabbed the door to the bathroom to steady herself. 'And to think that just for a moment there I thought you were a nice guy who didn't want me found dead on my own in the house.' Her light tone painted a thin veneer over the hurt. 'You should have talked to me before you went to all that trouble. I could have told you that it won't make any difference to my father. I could be in Intensive Care and he still wouldn't come.'

His dark brows were already locked in a deep frown as he digested her emotional confession. 'You're saying that your father would see the news that you're in hospital and still not get in touch?'

His appalled response drove her mood lower still. If there was one thing worse than having a parent who didn't care, it was the world knowing about it.

Why on earth had she told him that much?

It was the headache, she thought miserably. 'Look, just leave me alone. I've had enough of you to last me a lifetime. I hope your conscience doesn't keep you awake.'

He stared at her for a long moment and it was obvious he wanted to say more. Instead, his mouth tightened. 'Don't lock the door. If you collapse, I want to know.'

'Why? So that you can call the paparazzi and have them take close-ups?' Feeling worse than she'd ever felt in her life, Polly stalked into the bathroom, slammed the door and defiantly turned the key in the lock.

Damn.

Discovering that tears stung the cut next to her eye, she

ground her teeth and held back the emotion, knowing that a crying fit would simply add to her throbbing headache.

'Miserable man—vile, inhuman machine—' Venting in front of the mirror, she wet the corner of a towel and gingerly touched her head. 'Oww.' Gritting her teeth, she tried to analyse why she felt so let down. She was used to looking out for herself, wasn't she? She'd always done it. She didn't *need* Damon Doukakis flying to her rescue.

So why did she feel so let down? Why did it matter that his reasons for dumping his date to come and find her had been self-serving?

Polly stared at her white face in the mirror.

Because, just for a moment, she'd been taken in by those distracting flashes of chemistry. Just for a moment she'd forgotten this was all about his sister and made the mistake of thinking he cared about her a little bit.

That was what you got for dropping your guard.

Trying to ignore the pain, she took her time in the bathroom, wanting to make sure he'd gone before she emerged.

When she finally opened the door, the room was empty.

On the bed was a suitcase, presumably packed with the clothes she'd put on the list.

Fantastic Franco obviously worked fast.

On the table next to the bed were painkillers and a jug of water.

Polly sniffed, determined not to be grateful. Delivering painkillers didn't make him thoughtful.

She swallowed them and then pulled on the lacy shorts and camisole she wore to bed, trying not to think about the serious-faced Franco packing her clothes. Digging out her BlackBerry from her bag, she checked her e-mails. Having satisfied herself that there was nothing that couldn't wait until the morning, she settled on top of the bed, pulled out her notebook and started to scribble down thoughts for the following day's meeting. Determined to show Gérard that he'd done the right thing appointing them as his agency, she sketched out a few new ideas until drowsiness got the better of her and she flopped back onto the pillows.

His hand locked around a glass of whisky, Damon watched the news report from the hospital. There were stills of Polly being lifted into an ambulance, blood visible on her face, and an interview with the doctor who refused to comment on her patient's condition. It was enough to drive to most laid-back parent to the nearest telephone.

But the phone remained ominously silent.

What would it take, he wondered, to flush Peter Prince out of his love nest? Clearly more than an injured daughter.

What sort of man saw that his daughter was in hospital and still didn't call her?

Contemplating that question, Damon drained the whisky. Responsibility towards family flowed through him, as much a part of his being as the blood that was his life force. He could no more abdicate that responsibility than he could stop breathing.

From the moment the police had broken the news about his parents he'd buried his own feelings and focused all his energies on providing for his sister.

Clearly Peter Prince felt no such sense of obligation.

Damon thought back to that day a decade earlier when he'd received the call from the school. He'd walked out of an important meeting to go to his sister and, yes, he'd given her a hard time. Children, especially teenagers, needed rules and discipline. But his abiding memory of that day wasn't anything to do with Arianna. It was of Polly Prince, standing in one corner of the office, alone and defiant as he'd torn strips off her. *Alone.* There had been no sign of her father. At the time,

Damon had taken that evidence of lax parenting to be the reason his daughter had slid so far off the rails.

Now he was wondering whether 'lax' should be replaced with 'absent'.

Just what part had the man played in Polly's life?

His phone buzzed. As he answered the call Damon glanced towards the guest room but the door remained firmly closed and he wondered uneasily if he should have checked on her again. The doctor had told him she needed someone around.

Trying to block out an unsettling image of Polly stretched unconscious on the floor of the guest bathroom, he spoke to his pilot an then terminated the call and considered his options.

Of course she wasn't unconscious.

The girl was tougher than Kevlar.

But the image stayed with him as he gave a soft curse and strode through the apartment towards the guest suite. *One look*, he promised himself. As long as she was breathing, he'd leave her alone.

Pushing open the door, he saw her curled up in a ball on top of the bed, a notebook face down on the white silk cover, ink from a discarded pen spreading black blotches across the delicate fabric.

But it wasn't the ink that caught his attention. It was the exceptional pallor of her face. Remembering the doctor's comment that she should have stayed in hospital, he crossed the room swiftly, his overriding emotion one of concern. Was the wound bleeding again? He gently pushed her hair away from her face and the soft strands flowed over his hand like liquid gold, the scent of it distracting him from his purpose.

Reminding himself that he was supposed to be checking her head, he stroked her hair back and studied her face.

There were dark violet shadows under her eyes and the

livid bruise on her forehead was an angry smudge. Asleep, she looked younger than ever.

How did she feel, he wondered, knowing that her father didn't care enough to call?

Staring down at her, he remembered the words she'd thrown at him in the boardroom.

'If there's an emergency, I'm expected to handle it.'

To her credit, she'd been trying to handle it all day. Whatever he might think of the way he used office space, there was no denying that she'd worked hard to help settle the staff into their new surroundings and she'd defended them with a passion that had surprised him.

Wondering how anyone so small could be so monumentally aggravating, Damon gently removed the offending pen from her limp fingers and put it on the table next to the bed.

As he leaned forward and pulled the duvet over her, the pink notebook tumbled onto the floor.

Damon retrieved it, smoothed the crumpled pages, and was about to close it when something caught his eye.

Run, breathe, live.....

She'd scribbled the words over the pages of her notebook in scrawling, loopy handwriting but what caught his attention were the other combinations.

Run, live
Run right
Live to run
Feel alive

She'd obviously been playing with a million combinations in an attempt to come up with a tagline that worked for the brand.

His attention still fixed on the book, Damon sank onto the side of the bed. With no qualms about delving into her privacy, he flicked back to the beginning, reading what she'd written.

One thing stood out with startling, unsettling clarity.

He'd been completely and utterly wrong in his assessment of Polly Prince.

The creative brain behind every brilliant campaign belonged to the girl lying on the bed.

CHAPTER FIVE

POLLY woke to an insistent buzzing sound. Cracking open one eye, she was dazzled by an intense beam of light and she gave a moan and stuck her head under the pillow. 'Turn that spotlight off.'

'It's the sun.'

'Well, what's the sun doing up at this time?' Irritable, she stuck her head under the pillow and then howled with pain as it brushed against her wound. 'Ow. That hurts. And that noise is—'

'You set the alarm on your phone.' A strong bronzed hand appeared in front of her face and he picked up her BlackBerry and silenced the noise. 'It's six o'clock.'

'*Nooooo*. It can't be…' Her voice was muffled by the pillow. 'Go away.'

'You are welcome to turn over and go back to sleep, but you've slept without moving all night and I wanted to know you were alive.'

'I'm not alive. No one is ever truly alive at this hour of the morning.' She gave a whimper and huddled under the covers. 'Leave me alone.'

'You feel ill?' His voice was tight. 'I will call the doctor and ask him to come.'

'I don't need a doctor. I'm always like this in the morning whether I've banged my head or not. I'm not a morning person. I have to wake up slowly in my own time. What are you doing in my room anyway? I suppose you're sitting there planning new methods to use me to flush my father out of hiding. I'm just a worm on a hook.' All the horrors of the night before rushed down on her and Polly touched her fingers to her forehead. 'Did you put your hook through my head?'

'No, but that's still on my list of possible actions.' He sounded exasperated. 'Just for the record, I'm in your room because I was worried about you.'

'How long have you been there?'

'Most of the night. I slept in the chair. I wanted to be sure you didn't develop any of the signs the doctor mentioned.'

Carefully, so that she didn't brush her wound again, Polly cautiously removed the pillow and looked at him. Some time during the night he'd changed out of his tuxedo, discarded his bloodstained shirt and showered. Casually dressed in black jeans and a polo shirt, he looked every bit as striking as he did in a suit.

'You don't look like a guy who slept in a chair.' He looked sickeningly energetic, she thought gloomily, resentful at being forced to start her day confronted by all that vibrant masculinity. 'You watched me sleeping? Isn't that a little creepy?'

'It's boring. You're not very exciting when you're asleep.' Despite the mockery in his tone, his words jarred uncomfortably with the forbidden thoughts she'd been having.

'So why did you watch me? Were you afraid your hostage might die?'

'You are *not* my hostage.'

'You brought me here so because you're hoping my father will come and find me, not because you care about me, so stop the saint act. That makes me your hostage.'

Stunned by the discovery that he'd spent the night watching over her, Polly sat up slowly and noticed the cup of coffee on the low table next to the bed. The aroma of fresh coffee seduced her brain, sliding underneath her defences. 'Oh—is that for me?'

'Yes. I'm fast learning that your preference is for pink, but I'm afraid I don't own a pink cup.'

She didn't know which irritated her more—his dry tone, or the fact that he radiated vitality while she felt like a wet rag.

'Of course you don't. You're the sort of man who has to constantly prove his masculinity by bossing everyone around. A real man isn't afraid to have pink in his life. It's a very happy colour. Real men often wear pink ties or pink shirts.'

'Real men?' His sardonic smile was the final straw and she glared at him over the rim of the mug.

'Yes. And by that I don't mean all that muscle and testosterone stuff. ' Her eyes dropped to the hint of dark stubble that was already shadowing his jaw. 'Masculinity isn't just about looking as if you can split a log with one swing of an axe.' Which he did. Oh, God, how could a man look so incredibly good first thing in the morning? Particularly after he'd slept in a chair. Stubble on most men just looked unkempt. On Damon Doukakis it simply amplified his ferocious sex appeal. It wasn't fair.

'I've split logs in my time, but I confess I've never done it wearing a pink shirt.'

Assailed by an unsettling image of those broad shoulders swinging an axe, Polly was about to put the mug down when she spotted the ink on the bedcover. 'Oh, *no*! Did I do that? I'm so sorry. I must have fallen asleep holding my pen.'

'Your pink, fluffy, happy pen. The one that is necessary for all your creative thinking.'

Something in his tone didn't sound quite right but Polly was too mortified by the damage she'd caused to work out what. She licked her finger and rubbed at the stain. When that didn't work, she looked at him apologetically. 'I'll buy you another duvet cover. I know you have a low opinion of me but damage to property isn't on my usual list of crimes. I really *am* sorry.'

'Compared to most of the disasters that appear to happen when you are around, I would say I escaped lightly. Get dressed. I want to talk to you.'

'What have I done this time?'

'That's what I intend to find out.'

Polly racked her brains to think of something he could have discovered that might have got her into trouble. Was this something about the way they'd decorated the office? 'It's not a great time to talk right now. I need to get going if I'm going to make my train to Paris.'

'A moment ago you were all but unconscious. You're not going to Paris.'

'I slept like the dead because I'm really tired, not because I banged my head. I haven't slept properly since you rang me to tell me that you were about to ruin my life. And I *have* to go to Paris. The staff are depending on me to keep that account.' Trying to wake herself up, Polly pushed her hair away from her face and winced as she encountered the bruise. 'If I hurry, I can still make it.'

'Why are you so determined to protect the staff?'

'What sort of a question is that? Because I care about them, that's why. I don't want them to lose their jobs—especially because part of the blame for the current mess lies with my father. I feel responsible. They've always been kind to me. And helpful. When I first started in the company I'd just left school—I was clueless.'

'You didn't go to university?'

Polly thought wistfully of the prospectuses they'd shredded. 'I went straight to work in my father's company when I left school. I learned on the job. You can learn a lot about something by doing it.' Knowing that someone like him was never going to agree with her, she slumped back against the pillows. 'Anything else you want to know?'

Her notebook landed on the bed next to her and she stared

at it, her cheeks hot as she mentally ran through all the secrets that might have been revealed from that book.

He waited a beat. 'Well?'

'Well, what?'

'It made for extremely illuminating bedtime reading.'

'It's very bad manners to read someone else's private notes,' she said in a small voice. 'I suppose you also peep through keyholes and listen at doors.'

'Yesterday I asked you who came up with the creative ideas. Why didn't you just tell me the truth?'

'I told you it was a team effort. That's the truth.'

'The tagline and thinking behind the running shoe campaign came from you. If this notebook is to be believed, you're responsible for every decent creative idea that has come from Prince Advertising in the past three years. I've been looking through the portfolio and your company accounts—'

Polly flinched. 'More bedtime reading? You obviously like a good horror story.'

'More like a mystery. My financial director, Ellen, has unpicked the finances and those numbers make for interesting reading. Why did everyone agree to take such a drastic pay cut?'

'You have a *female* financial director?'

'Don't change the subject.'

'Why did we take a pay cut? Because no one wanted anyone to be made redundant. Close your eyes while I find something decent to wear. You're right, I can't have this sort of conversation in my pyjamas.' Sliding out of bed, Polly grabbed something from her suitcase and shot towards the bathroom. 'As I said, we're a team. We're in this together.'

'You clearly have significant creative talent. Why wasn't it recognised?'

The compliment stopped her in her tracks. Her smile faltered. 'You think I have talent?'

'Answer my question.'

Holding the clothes in front of her like a shield, she shrugged. 'You met the board.'

'When you hinted that they'd stolen your work, I assumed you were talking about the spreadsheets.'

Polly just looked at him and he sighed.

'They claimed credit for all your ideas, didn't they? When they pitched for business, you were part of the team?'

'I had to be. No one on the board was able to present the ideas. So they went along as the figurehead and I did the talking.'

'And you won High Kick Hosiery.' He shook his head in disbelief. 'We should have won that account.'

'We were better. Which just goes to show that even a hot desk doesn't always produce hot ideas. And now, if you'll excuse me, I have a train to catch.' The mere thought of battling her way through the train station made her want to lie down in a dark room, but she'd rather walk to Paris in bare feet than admit that to him.

'You're not travelling on a train. A doctor will examine you and then if he says you're fit to fly then we'll go to Paris on my jet.'

'Your jet? Er—why?'

'Because I don't travel by train.'

'No, I mean—' She licked her lips. 'Why are *you* coming? I'm assuming you're not joining me for a romantic mini-break.' She hoped that being flippant would break the tension between them.

It didn't.

He was obviously as aware of it as she was because he narrowed his eyes.

'I make you nervous. Why?'

Her stomach curled and her mouth dried. What was she

supposed to say to that? *Because you have monumental sex appeal.* 'You're the boss. You can fire me.'

His eyes held hers. 'That isn't why you're nervous.'

Wondering why she was such a mess when it came to men, Polly gave what she hoped was a dismissive shrug. 'Look, there's a lot going on, OK? Gérard's business is important. He has one of the largest marketing budgets in Europe. It's not just about this brand, it's about the rest of his portfolio. If I do well in this meeting, he might give us more business.'

'That's why I'm coming with you. You shouldn't be seeing someone of his seniority on your own.'

'You mean you don't trust me not to mess it up.'

'On the contrary. I want to watch you in action. I want to know more about your novel creative process.' Infuriatingly calm, he glanced at his watch. 'Get dressed. We'll finish this discussion later.'

'Well, that's something to look forward to. Yippee.' She subsided as he shot her a warning look.

He walked towards the door and then paused. 'You ought to know that an hour ago I had a call from the private investigator I hired to track your father. It seems that he's also in Paris.'

'Oh?' Was it wrong not to be pleased that he'd been tracked down? Her mouth was dry and she wondered whether it was the bang on the head that was making her feel sick or whether it was the thought of weathering the reality of her father's next relationship. And this time it would be worse because the woman in question was Arianna. Her friend. Damon's sister 'He could be in Paris. My father is a romantic person.'

'There is nothing romantic about a relationship between a fifty-four-year-old guy and a twenty-four-year-old girl.'

'You don't know that. You're very judgemental.'

'When it comes to protecting my family, yes, I'm judge mental.' His voice was suddenly hard. 'And, talking o judgemental, I hope you put 'formal business wear' on the list you gave Franco. If you're going to take on the responsibility of a high-flying business executive then you need to look like one. You may be used to flouncing into work in party clothes, but if you're meeting a vice president of marketing you need to clean up your image. The French appreciate chic. The look you should be going for is high-class and elegant.'

Smug in the knowledge that there was so much more he yet had to discover about her, Polly couldn't resist a dig of her own. 'Is that how your team was dressed when they *didn't* win the pitch? You're very traditional. Maybe the client didn't want traditional. He said he was blown away by our creativity and individuality.'

'Presumably he wasn't referring to your appearance.'

Polly gave an innocent smile. 'Or maybe he just has a thing for flamingos. I'll get dressed and meet you in the living room. I need to make some calls before we leave. And for goodness' sake get changed into something more rigid and formal. I'm not taking you to Paris wearing those jeans.' Without giving him the chance to reply, she escaped into the bathroom and bolted the door.

'This is the wrong hotel. I booked myself somewhere cheap and miserable.' Prepared for something seedy, Polly blinked at the glamour and elegance of the luxurious hotel foyer. After seeing the inside of Damon's private jet she'd thought that nothing could ever impress her again. Evidently she'd been wrong. 'Unless the place has had a major upgrade in the past twenty-four hours, this definitely isn't the place I chose.' Light shafted off gold, marble and glass and every person who glided through the revolving doors looked like a multi-millionaire. A sense of inferiority nibbled the edges of her confidence and she stood up a little straighter and tried to look as if she belonged.

No matter how many times she told herself that she deserved to be here she still felt like a fake. It depressed her that she could still feel that way.

The moment Damon set foot in the exclusive hotel there was a subtle shift in the atmosphere. Heads turned, staff straightened uniforms and descended on him with just the right degree of discretion and deference. Smiles were plentiful. Nothing was too much trouble.

Accustomed to staying in cheap hotels, checking in with grumpy, overworked staff and hauling her ancient suitcase up endless stairs only to find herself in an airless room with a window overlooking a grim car park, Polly was fascinated by the contrast.

The staff were attentive to the point of smothering. Damon's presence had an electrifying effect on those around him. He barely acknowledged them, accepting the fawning attention with the same arrogant assurance he displayed in every other part of his life.

This was his normal.

'I can't afford to stay here.' Seriously worried, Polly was mentally running through the budget. 'I could never charge this to the client.'

'I think we both know that finances aren't your strong point. From now on you can leave that side of the business to me. You just concentrate on the creative side, which apparently is your forte.' Leaving his security team to sort out the details with the hotel staff, Damon strode through the foyer. 'I've booked out a floor for us.'

A floor? 'Could you slow down? Just wait a minute.' Worried that her 'creative side' might have gone on vacation, Polly jogged to keep up with him as he strode towards a bank of elevators. 'I can't ignore the finances. I have to think about it.'

'You're the one who mentioned teamwork. This is teamwork. We each do the bit we do best. For you, that's scribbling in your pink notebook. Leave the money to me.'

'Yes, but—' Her phone buzzed and she paused outside the elevator. 'Wait a minute. I need to answer this… *Bonjour, Gérard, ça va? Oui…d'accord…*' When she finally finished her call, Damon was standing inside the elevator, watching her through those thick, dusky lashes that tipped his looks from handsome to spectacular.

Her heart skittered and bumped as she joined him. 'Sorry about that, but I couldn't exactly put a VP of marketing on hold.'

'I didn't expect you to put him on hold. I also didn't expect you to speak French.'

'There's a lot you don't know about me. I have hidden talents.'

'So I'm discovering.' That disturbingly acute gaze didn't shift from her face. 'You haven't stopped e-mailing and talking to people since you woke up. When did you learn to speak French?'

'We had a seriously hot French master at school. It was the only lesson we were all awake in—' Remembering too late that mentioning school probably wasn't a good idea, Polly flushed. 'Just kidding. I promised myself that if a gorgeous Frenchman ever whispered sweet nothings in my ear I wanted to be able to understand him.'

'If he's whispering nothing it would probably be better not to understand him,' Damon said dryly and his words made her laugh.

Then she realised she was laughing and stopped instantly. But the connection remained. A connection she didn't want or need and yet still it sucked her in, driving her heartbeat faster. The sudden darkening of his beautiful eyes told her he felt it too and rejected the unwanted chemistry as completely as she did. Perversely, that rejection didn't hurt as much as aggravate. Her emotions spun and suddenly she wanted to press her mouth to his and kiss away the sarcasm and cynicism that flowed from him.

The impulse was so alien to her that if she'd been in possession of a thermometer she would have taken her own temperature. *Was she ill?*

Alarmed by her own thoughts, Polly was relieved when they reached the palatial suite.

'*C'est magnifique.*' Grateful for the size of it, she walked the length of the spacious living room and out thought the open glass doors to the roof terrace. The fresh air brushed away the claustrophobic cloud that had smothered her in the confines of the lift. That crazy impulse to kiss him faded and she breathed a sigh of relief as she stared over the rooftops of Paris. Enjoying the moment of relative calm, she tensed as she heard his footsteps behind her.

'Where would your father stay?'

'He'd stay somewhere no one would think to look for him. That's the sort of guy he is.' Thinking wistfully that it would be nice to enjoy the luxury of the hotel and the romance of Paris without having to think about work or her father, Polly turned from her contemplation of the city. 'This isn't just about my father, you know. It's also about your sister. She hasn't been on the phone to you, has she? That sort of implies that she doesn't want to be found.'

'She's very impulsive and easily led.'

Polly clenched her jaw. 'If you're still going on about that episode at school, can I remind you that I was fourteen? That was ten years ago. She's an adult now.'

'She doesn't behave like an adult. She doesn't always make good decisions.'

'Isn't that part of growing up? You have to make some bad decisions in order to discover they're bad.' Polly attributed the sudden warm flush on her skin to the hot French sun shining down on the terrace. 'Didn't you ever make a bad decision? Or were you born doing the right thing? I suppose life just fell into place for you.'

The fruits of that success were all around him. Not just in this hotel and the private jet that had transported them to Paris in such luxury, but in his lifestyle. He owned an island in Greece, didn't he? A penthouse in New York and a ski chalet in Switzerland. People fell over themselves to befriend Damon Doukakis and his sister. They walked through life without hindrance, doors swinging open to welcome them.

'You think I was born into this? You think I had it handed to me?' His voice held a raw, rough edge that increased her tension. 'My father worked for an engineering company. A badly managed engineering company. When he was made redundant, he was so ashamed that he'd let his family down that every morning he kissed my mother goodbye and left to go to work. Only instead of going to work he used to sit in the library and hunt for jobs. But there weren't any.'

Shocked into silence by that unexpected revelation, Polly simply stared at him. When she finally managed to say something it came out as a croak. 'D-did he get another job?'

'No. My father was Greek. Proud. Not being able to provide for his family was the ultimate failure. Overwhelmed with the responsibility of it, he drove his car off a bridge.' The words were emotionless and matter of fact. 'I was waiting for them to come home when the police knocked on the door.'

Polly couldn't breathe. 'Them?'

'My mother was in the car, too. No one understood why he did it. Whether he lost all hope and decided to take her with him—whether she even knew what he intended—' His eyes were blank as he stared over the city. 'Do you know the worst thing? The redundancies weren't necessary. I found that out a few years later when I'd learned a few sharp lessons about business. It was all down to bad decisions and I decided right then that I was never going to work for anyone else. I was never going to let someone else control my destiny.'

It explained so much. His ruthless approach. The rigid control with which he managed his business.

Polly realised that her impression of him was as false as his was of her.

It was as if the pieces of a jigsaw had been thrown in the air and, on landing, had created a different picture.

'You were left to raise your sister.'

'She was six.' He gave a wry smile. 'I was sixteen years old and the only skill I had was with computers. I was always in trouble at school for hacking, so I decided there had to be a way of turning that to my advantage. I developed a way of analysing data that every company wanted.' He shrugged. 'Right place, right time. I was lucky.'

'But your business isn't computers now—'

'Something else I learned—diversify. That way if one part of the business is in trouble, another part may be performing well.'

He'd thought it all through. Done everything he could to provide security for his sister.

Feeling a strange ache behind her ribcage, Polly turned away. She shouldn't envy someone who had suffered such a tragic loss, but she did. Even without parents, they'd been a family. Everything he'd done, everything he'd achieved, had been driven by his love for Arianna. Protecting her had been his priority from the moment she'd been left in his care.

'It must have been very hard losing both your parents like that.'

'Life can be hard. It happens.' He glanced towards her, his expression unreadable. 'What happened to your mother? Presumably she was divorce number one?'

The ache behind her ribs didn't fade. 'She walked out when I was a toddler. Being a mother didn't suit her. Or maybe I was just hard work. Whichever—my dad hated being on his own. Whenever a relationship fell apart, he moved onto the next woman.'

Even now, at twenty-four, she found her father's behaviour still had the power to embarrass her and she hated that. She hated the mixed-up feelings that came with every new relationship he started.

'The women are always younger?'

Hearing the judgement in his voice, Polly felt her face heat and wanted to fall through the floor. 'Mostly.'

'Is that embarrassing?'

'Hideous.' In the face of his startling honesty about his own background there didn't seem any point in lying about her feelings.

He let out a long breath. 'So you don't approve of his relationship with Ana?'

'You didn't ask me if I approved. You asked me if I found it embarrassing. The answer to that is yes. As for whether or not I approve—' She broke off, wondering why on earth she was sharing her deepest thoughts with this man whose opinion of her was so low. He couldn't possibly understand, could he? 'He's my dad and I love him. I just want him to be happy. Isn't that what you want for Arianna?'

'Yes, which is why I don't approve of this relationship.'

'I think all relationships are complicated and I'm not sure age makes any difference to that.'

'When you see a twenty-four-year old girl with a fifty-four year old man, don't you ask yourself why they're together?'

Polly chewed her lip, wondering whether to confess that the entire relationship merry-go-round terrified her. The whole thing seemed designed to wreck lives. 'This is the twenty-first century. Age of same-sex marriages, the toyboy and the cougar. Relationships don't always conform to rigid tradition any more. Why does it bother you? You're too big and tough to care what people think.' But Damon Doukakis was rigidly traditional. Greek. If she'd learned anything about him over the past twenty-four hours it was that family was the most important thing to him.

'I don't care what people think. I do care that Ana will be hurt. Let's face it, your father doesn't have a great track record when it comes to commitment.'

Polly made a weak attempt to defend him. 'You're not exactly famed for long-term commitment.'

'That's different.'

'You move from one woman to the next. Apart from the obvious—prenuptial agreements, huge payouts to lawyers etc—what's the difference?'

'Marriage is a responsibility and I have more than enough responsibilities.' He took a deep breath as if the mere thought of it was enough to unsettle him. 'In my relationships there are no broken promises. No one gets hurt.'

'For a woman not to care when a relationship ends, the man in question has either got to be incredibly boring or a real bastard. What I'm saying is that I'm pretty sure plenty of women get hurt when you dump them. They probably just don't show it. Pride and all that. And I don't really see the difference between your serial relationships and my father's. Not every relationship has to be about marriage.' But the fact that he felt so strongly about responsibility and commitment made her feel strange inside. It was so different from her father's approach.

'If you're about to say my sister's relationship with your father is about sex then don't,' he advised in a thickened tone. 'I don't want to think about that.'

'That makes two of us. He's my dad and no one wants to think about their parents having sex. Yuck.' Polly gave a dramatic shudder. 'But you have to admit that Arianna is an adult. My father hasn't kidnapped her against her will. They enjoy each other's company.'

His brow lifted in a cynical arch. 'Are you about to use the word "love"?

She didn't tell him that she didn't believe in love. She'd seen what happened to people who believed in love and she'd made it her golden rule never to allow herself to be sucked into that particular delusion. 'They get on well together,' she said lamely. 'They laugh all the time. They talk. There's chemistry between them. Maybe they know it's crazy but find it impossible to resist.'

'Chemistry?' There was an ominous pause and she could see the thought appalled him. His eyes locked on hers and suddenly thoughts of her father and his sister faded into the background. In the distance she heard the insistent cacophony of car horns, the shriek of tyres as Parisians drove their city like a racetrack, but the loudest sound was the insistent thrumming of her pulse.

Suddenly it was hard to keep a grip on the conversation. 'Chemistry,' she croaked. 'I'm just saying that chemistry can be a powerful thing.' Or so she'd heard. Truthfully she couldn't imagine a sexual attraction so strong that it overpowered caution but she wasn't going to admit that to a red-blooded male whose sexual prowess was the subject of hushed rumour. 'Perhaps it was something they couldn't walk away from. I don't know.'

There was a long silence and then his strong hands captured her face and he lowered his mouth to hers. Caught off guard, Polly tumbled headlong into the addictive heat of his kiss, her mouth colliding with his in a fusion of intimacy that was shocking in its intensity. The exploding heat was fierce enough to fuel a nuclear reactor, the hunger so all-consuming it devoured her preconceptions about just how a kiss could feel because this kiss was like no other. Damon kissed the way he did everything else, with the instinctive assurance of someone who knew he was the very best at everything. That clever, sensuous mouth drove everything from her mind and he controlled it all, from the angle of her head to the depth of the kiss, the skilled erotic slide of his tongue taking over her mind, her body, her soul. She didn't feel him move his hands but he must have done because suddenly she was flattened against his hard thighs, the contours of their bodies blending as fiery heat licked through her. Burning up, she slid her palms over his chest, feeling male muscle and latent strength. Her mouth still fused with his, she slid her fingers between the buttons of his shirt, desperate to touch, frantic to feel. Instantly his hand tightened on her bottom as he brought her into firm contact with the hard ridge of his erection.

Liquid with longing, Polly moved against him but the moment she did so he released his grip on her and lifted his mouth, depriving her of the satisfaction her body craved. And that sudden deprivation was so sharply felt that she gave a faint moan of protest and swayed towards him. With a soft curse he locked his hands around the tops of her arms, holding her steady, as if he sensed she would not stay standing without his support. But he kept the distance and didn't kiss her again. Slowly, the implications of that penetrated her foggy brain and she opened her eyes to find him watching her with those eyes as black as jet and unfathomable as a deep mountain pool.

Her body was screaming for more, refusing to adjust to the sudden withdrawal of pleasure. The craving was so intense she almost reached out and grabbed him just so that she could press her mouth to his again. She wanted to know why he'd stopped doing something that felt so perfect.

His breathing fractionally less than steady, he released his supporting grip on her arms and stepped away from her. 'You want to know how you walk away from chemistry? This is how it's done. It's called self-discipline. You just say no.' The chill in his tone was as lethal to her tender, exposed feelings as a late frost to an early spring bud.

Confronted by cool arrogance and an insulting degree of indifference, Polly wanted to say something flippant. Something dismissive that would indicate that the earth hadn't moved for her. But it had. It hadn't just moved, it had shifted—reformed her entire emotional landscape into something terrifyingly unfamiliar. And that shift strangled any words she might have spoken.

She wanted to slap his handsome face, but to show that level of emotion would be to betray what that kiss had done to her so she stood still and silent, holding everything inside. Fortunately she'd had decades of practice.

Insultingly cool, Damon glanced at his watch. 'We're meeting Gérard for dinner at the Eiffel Tower at seven.' The ease with which he moved from nirvana to normal was another blow to her savaged pride. 'Dress is elegant.' Having delivered that lowering statement, he turned and walked back into the apartment—back into his world of pampered luxury and elegance where real life was filtered and sifted until it appeared in its most refined form.

Polly stood for a moment feeling displaced. Really, what had just happened? She was the same and yet she wasn't the same. Opening her mouth a fraction, she traced her lower lip with her tongue.

Her first thought was that clearly the kiss hadn't affected him as it had affected her, and yet she knew that wasn't true. She'd felt the strength of his reaction.

However easily he'd walked away, it had definitely been mutual.

He'd kissed her to prove—what? That he could walk away every time? That lust was a decision like every other? She wondered whether the intensity of the chemistry had been as much of a shock to him as it was to her.

Anger flashed through her. How dared he kiss like that and then just walk away?

No doubt he was feeling smug and superior, having successfully demonstrated the practical application of ruthless self control, whereas she—Polly breathed in and out slowly—she'd demonstrated nothing except an embarrassing degree of feminine compliance. Compelled by his breathtaking sexual expertise, she'd been ready to go the whole way. Like Icarus, she would have flown straight at that hot burning sun, the ecstasy of the flight obliterating any sense of caution.

In proving his point, he'd made a monumental fool of her.

Furious and humiliated, she turned her head and looked back towards the luxurious suite, but there was no sign of him. Presumably, having achieved his goal with such spectacular success, he'd taken himself off somewhere to focus his sought-after attentions on some aspect of his global empire before the meeting this evening. A meeting during which he was clearly expecting her to embarrass him.

Dress is elegant.

He thought she was going to mess up.

Polly's mouth tightened.

She *knew* how good she was at her job. If only she were half as good in her dealings with men he wouldn't have played that trick on her. So far he'd made nothing but false assumptions and she'd been so focused on handling the immediate crisis that she'd done nothing to challenge him on his opinions.

But tonight that was going to change.

If Damon Doukakis thought he could control everything around him then he was in for a shock.

CHAPTER SIX

'I'LL lead the meeting.' Damon sprawled in the back of the limo, grateful for a stack of e-mails that gave him a legitimate excuse to limit social contact with the woman next to him. An expanse of soft leather seat stretched between them like no man's land as they both kept a wary distance.

Why on earth had he revealed so much about himself?

'Why would you lead the meeting when you weren't the one who won the pitch.' Her tone was cool and when he risked a glance at her he saw that she was also on her BlackBerry, her slim fingers were flying over the keys with enviable dexterity as she responded to an e-mail. Not once did she look at him and Damon frowned, unaccustomed to such a lack of interest from a woman, especially a woman he'd kissed.

'It makes sense that I'll lead the discussion. I've known Gérard for fifteen years.'

'Oh, I see. It's the boys' club approach. No worries. You just carry on and beat your chests and do all that masculine stuff, and when you've finished I'll present my ideas.'

Damon didn't know which infuriated him more—her words, or the fact that she didn't bother looking up as she spoke them.

'The way I conduct a business meeting has nothing to do with the "boys' club".' He chose to ignore the anatomical reference.

'There's no need to be defensive. You don't have to apologise for feeling the need to be the dominant male in every situation. I'm sure that basic flaw has proved fundamental to your success in business.'

'Are you calling masculinity a *flaw*?'

'Gosh, no. Not masculinity.' Her fingers flew over the keys swiftly. 'Just dominant controlling tendencies that prevent you from ever thinking another person with a different approach could be saying something worth hearing.'

Damon's jaw ached from clenching his teeth. 'I am always very receptive to fresh ideas.'

'Providing they're coming from someone dressed in a dark suit. Be honest—you took one look at me and dismissed me on the basis of my dress and my pink tights.'

'That is *not* true.'

'It is true. And once we're in the restaurant the first thing you'll discuss is the success of each other's businesses, your various achievements and how many financial goals you've scored. He'll acknowledge you as King of the Jungle, you'll order an eye-wateringly expensive bottle of wine to prove your impeccable taste and his importance as a client, and once we've got all that alpha male posturing out of the way I can have my turn.'

Damon breathed deeply. 'You're being intentionally confrontational. You're upset because I kissed you.'

That got her attention.

She glanced up. Her brows rose. 'Why would that upset me? You're a good kisser. No woman is going to object to being kissed by a man who knows what he's doing. Although you might want to work on the ending—it was a bit abrupt. But better that than slobbery.' Having delivered what she clearly considered to be useful feedback, she returned to her phone. 'So—back to this meeting of ours. I just need to make sure I understand the ground rules. You need to have control of everything you do, and that's fine. I don't have a problem with that. I'll take a back seat until you've finished with the whole ego-massaging thing.'

Still grappling with her matter-of-fact response to the kiss, Damon found himself unable to respond.

He wondered whether her choice of long coat had anything to do with her rejection of what had happened earlier. It covered everything from her neck to her ankles, leaving no part of her uncovered. There was nothing sexual about her appearance. Nothing provocative. Which made the fact that he wanted to haul her across that void all the more unfathomable and aggravating. His fingers burned to reach out and grab her, rip open those buttons and feast on the flavours he'd sampled earlier.

Acutely aware that he was entirely to blame for his current condition, Damon employed the last of his willpower and transferred his gaze from her face to the window. It was a mistake. Paris in darkness sparkled and glittered like a film set and lovers walked hand in hand along the banks of the Seine, creating memories that would be stored for a lifetime. Everything about the night suggested intimacy.

Exasperated by the direction of his thoughts, Damon turned his attention back to his phone, forced to admit that in an attempt to prove his self-control he'd found himself severely tested. Yes, he'd won. He always made sure he won whatever battle he fought. But it had required a strength of will he'd never before needed to apply to that type of situation.

When his driver pulled up close to the Eiffel Tower, Damon made a swift, smooth exit, relieved to be released from the claustrophobic confines of the car.

Polly emerged slowly and stood a safe distance away from him. 'This seems an odd venue for a dinner meeting. I hope you didn't misunderstand.' She stared at the long queue of people waiting for the opportunity to go up to the top of the tower.

'Gérard is trying to impress you.' Damon noticed that this time the silky soft blonde hair had been twisted into a formal up do—severe rather than sexy. The sheen on her lips suggested a faint gloss but nothing too provocative. In fact, her entire appearance was understated. And her shoes were flat—perfect for cobbled Paris streets.

Clearly she'd paid attention to his instruction for 'elegant'.

He waited to relax—for the strange tightness to leave his body.

It didn't happen.

'I've dined here before. The restaurant is up there.'

She followed his gaze and tilted her head, looking up at the iconic landmark, its metal latticework turned to gold by hundreds of tiny lights, the famous structure standing proud again the spectacular Paris sunset. 'Gérard certainly knows how to impress a girl. Or was this your idea? Maybe this is all part of your God complex—you just have to be looking down on everyone else.'

Ignoring that remark, Damon urged her forward towards the private elevator reserved for those dining in the restaurant. Bringing a personal note to their relationship had been a mistake, he thought grimly. Thank goodness the evening would be about business. He and Gérard would discuss the transition of Prince Advertising into DMG and Polly could fill in any blanks on the previous management of the account and expand on her creative ideas for the brand.

As the elevator rose through the iconic building Damon kept his eyes forward. He was aware of Polly fidgeting beside him but he didn't turn his head, determined this time to keep his focus.

As they emerged into the restaurant they were met by the *maître d'* and by Gérard himself, who had evidently arrived just moments before them.

Long-time acquaintances and sparring partners, Damon

and the Frenchman greeted each other warmly while the front of house staff took Polly's coat. Deep in conversation about the strength of the euro, it took Damon a few moments to realise that he had lost his audience. Gérard's thoughts on currency fluctuations had clearly been sublimated by some higher priority that could only be female. Amused and exasperated in equal degrees, Damon turned his head to see who could have caused that degree of distraction.

His attention arrested by the woman behind him, it took him a moment to realise that it was Polly, minus the coat that she'd handed to the hovering staff. In the few seconds he'd had his back to her she'd gone from understated to unbelievable.

Transfixed by the dramatic transformation, Damon suddenly understood why she'd chosen to cover herself from head to foot. Had he seen her outfit he would have locked her in their hotel suite and thrown away the key. Abiding by his instruction to dress elegantly, she'd chosen to wear a black suit, but all hint of compliance ended with the colour. The tailored jacket was fastened by a single shapely button. A hint of black lace camisole was peeping naughtily from under the V of the lapels. The skirt was short, her legs showcased in a pair of exotic black stockings that shimmered and glistened in the candlelight. Mesmerised by those incredible legs, Damon saw that the shimmer was created by a pattern of tiny hearts embroidered in glittering silver thread and spiralling up from ankle to thigh.

They were cheeky and sexy and perfect for a hot date. Which made them completely unsuitable for a client meeting in his opinion.

'*Mademoiselle est ravissant.*' Apparently disagreeing with him, Gérard took her hand in a typically Gallic gesture and lifted it to his lips. 'Once again I am impressed. Your decision to showcase the jewel in our new product range in this high-profile venue is yet more proof that I was right to hire you. I love these. They are my favourite and I consider myself a connoisseur.'

Both of them looked down at her legs and Damon felt his core temperature rocket to dangerous levels. He was about to snap something when he realised they were talking about the tights, not her legs.

'I love them.' Polly beamed up at Gérard, paying Damon no attention whatsoever. 'They're special, sexy and so affordable. They can transform a plain boring black suit with no originality whatsoever—' her eyes flickered briefly to Damon '—into an outfit that makes any woman feel like a princess. They're the perfect day-to-night accessory and what's more they're within the budget of every discerning woman. I adore them. All the girls in the office are crazy for them. They're so very *now*.' The corners of her mouth dimpled as she smiled up at the captivated Frenchman. 'We're going to make sure they're the next big thing.'

'And you have ideas for me about how to turn that adoration into a worldwide campaign that will propel High Kick Hosiery into the must-have fashion statement of the decade?'

'Tons of ideas.' Reaching into her bag, Polly pulled out her pink notebook and waved it under Gérard's nose.

The notoriously hard-nosed businessman laughed indulgently. 'Ah, the famous notebook and even more famous pink pen. The deadly weapon with which Polly successfully defeats the opposition. Had Napoleon had you and your pink pen by his side, history would have been changed.' Smiling, he took her arm and led her towards the table. 'I want to hear your ideas. Given your love of pink, I'm surprised you didn't opt for our hot pink tights this evening.'

'Mr Doukakis isn't a lover of hot pink.' Balancing on impossibly high heels, Polly was almost as tall as the Frenchman. 'Apparently it makes him think of flamingos.'

Absorbing the fact that the hot pink tights had been another product in the High Kick Hosiery line, Damon wondered at what point his own agenda had obliterated his usual ability to think clearly. She'd chosen to showcase the sparkling tights at one of the most high-profile venues in Paris. Not only that, she'd worn the long black coat simply because she'd known he would have disapproved.

The fact that she could easily have told him she was wearing her client's products was something he'd raise with her later.

Poised to offer reassurance to Gérard on what the takeover would mean to his business, Damon found himself taking a back seat as Polly presented ideas for a global campaign— a campaign that left Damon speechless with its scope and creativity.

It slowly dawned on him that her contribution to the company was far greater than even his glimpse into her notebook had suggested.

Intercepting his stunned look, Gérard lifted his champagne glass. 'Incredible, isn't she?' There was a speculative look in his eyes as he looked at Polly. 'Much as it pains me to compliment a man whose ego is already robust, I salute Damon for his astute business sense in locking you into his company. Talented people are rare. With you, it is like finding a precious uncut diamond in a bucket of gravel. I admit that when my colleagues recommended that we invite Prince Advertising to pitch, I refused. But then the word spread about the girl with the pink pen and the creative brain. Only Damon Doukakis would be bold enough to take over an ailing company in order to secure one member of staff.'

Damon didn't correct him. 'She has some truly original ideas,' he agreed smoothly, 'and fortunately within the group we have the muscle to turn those big ideas into reality. We'll put out top team onto your account.'

'I don't care who is in the team.' Gérard dug his fork into

marinated scallops. 'I just want Polly. You're a crafty dog, Doukakis. I was about to recruit her myself.'

Reflecting on the news that Gérard had intended to offer Polly a job, Damon frowned, but Polly had abandoned her meal and was scribbling over her pad, absorbed by the ideas she was creating.

'We've plenty of time to agree tactics, but the overall strategy should establish the brand image. Then the emphasis needs to be on social media. It isn't just about getting across a message and selling, it's about relationship-building—engaging with our customer…I've got his brilliant idea for using YouTube—' Her suggestions were clever and intelligent and she charmed her client so completely that by the end of the meal he'd agreed to triple the budget and hear her ideas for two other major brands.

Damon watched her in action, unable to think of anything other than how her mouth had felt under his. His view of her as his baby sister's disruptive friend had somehow morphed into something dramatically different. He remembered the way she'd stood up to the board and challenged them. At the time he'd assumed her defence was driven by self-interest, but now he understood that her behaviour stemmed from the fact that she had a deep commitment to the people who worked for the company. Guilt stabbed him hard. It was gradually dawning on him that, far from being lazy, she worked every bit as hard as he did. She cared about the employees as much as he did. Even now, she was ignoring the throb in her head to honour a meeting with this important client when ninety nine percent of staff would have stayed in bed and called in sick.

Unaccustomed to being wrong about people, Damon was forced to admit that he'd allowed his anger with her father and his past experience of her to colour his judgement.

Brooding on how that could have happened, it took him

a few moments to notice that Gérard was increasingly attentive to Polly. Recognising sexual interest when he saw it, Damon felt a flare of outrage. When Gérard suggested ending the evening with a trip up to the viewing platform, Damon immediately vetoed that idea, appalled at the thought of the notorious French playboy accompanying Polly to a destination favoured by those seeking romance.

Shaken by the depth of that primal response, a devotee of rational, logical decision-making, Damon shocked himself by launching himself out of his seat and demanded their coats. It wasn't rational or logical, but he wanted her covered up as fast as possible. He wanted that coat back on, buttoned to the neck, concealing those amazing legs. The thought of the whole of Paris following the spiralling upward path of those tiny sparkling hearts made him sweat like a man running a marathon in a desert.

'We'll send you a full proposal in the next few days, Gérard.' Taking control, he ended the evening and then guided Polly back down to the waiting limo.

As his driver opened the door for them she stopped and shook her head. 'I want to go for a walk. It's been a horrible week and it's so beautiful here. It would be nice to get some air.' Behind her the Eiffel Tower was illuminated against the dark sky and he saw her glance wistfully towards the tourist attraction. 'You go. I can find my own way back to the hotel.' Balancing on one leg like a stork, she removed her stilettos and replaced them with her flats.

Knowing that if he left her alone for two minutes she would be mobbed by Frenchmen, Damon took the shoes from her, handed them to his driver and held out his arm.

Her gaze lifted from his arm to his face and he acknowledged her astonishment with a faint smile.

'Truce. I'm protecting my asset. Clearly I should have your pink pen insured for an astronomical amount.'

Her sudden smile knocked the breath from his body.

'I know I ought to do it all electronically, and I do once I know what I'm doing, but I just can't be creative on a screen—I need to draw. I was the same at school. The only way I remembered anything was by drawing spider diagrams and mind maps.'

She hesitated just briefly and then slid her arm through his. Dismissing his driver with a discreet movement of his head, Damon led her away from the crowds hovering at the foot of the iconic tower and across the road to the river. Strains of music and laughter drifted up from the *Bateaux mouches* as they floated under the bridge and Polly snuggled deeper inside her coat and stared down at the reflection of light on the water.

'I always wanted to stand on a bridge in Paris in the sunset.' There was a wistful note in her voice that drew his attention.

'But with a lover, not your enemy.'

'This may surprise you, but I don't dream of lovers, Mr Doukakis.' There was a brief pause and then she turned her head, the lights from the boat turning her hair to a gleaming shimmer of gold. 'And I don't see you as the enemy.'

Awareness throbbed between them and Damon inhaled deeply, feeling as though he were sinking in quicksand.

'You wanted to walk. Let's walk.' He carefully withdrew his arm and instead pushed his hands into the pocket of his coat to prevent himself from touching her. He'd always known that self-discipline began in the mind, but he was fast discovering his mind wasn't as strong as he'd previously thought. Maybe, he thought, he'd never been truly tested. He'd always avoided commitment of any sort, shying away from still more responsibility. He'd always made a point of keeping his relationships superficial and that was the way he wanted it to stay.

'You've been to Paris before?'

'No. This is the first time. When we pitched we went to their London offices.' She strolled next to him, her eyes back on the river. Light flickered on the rippling surface, a kaleidoscope of colour and texture reflected from the illuminated buildings that stretched along the banks of the Seine.

'It would have saved some misunderstanding had you revealed your level of input into the company right from the first moment. Clearly you were a key member of the team.'

'If I'd walked into the boardroom yesterday and told you that all the good ideas in the company were mine, would you have believed me?'

Damon breathed deeply. 'Possibly not. At least not initially. But you could have given me evidence.'

'I'd put together a presentation. No one would listen.'

'At the time I was handling the board, but when we were alone in the room afterwards you could have said something.'

'When, exactly? Before or after you told me to get my lazy self to work?' There was humour in her tone. 'I don't think you were exactly receptive.'

'*Theé mou*, stop turning me into the bad guy!'

'I'm just pointing out that you didn't exactly start out with a good opinion of me.' Her shoulders lifted in a tiny shrug. 'And I suppose I don't blame you for that. Because of me, your sister was excluded from school. And now she's run off with my dad. Which isn't exactly my fault, but I can see why it makes you angry to be near me.'

'I'm not angry. At least, not with you. I *am* frustrated that you didn't just tell me the truth about the company.'

'At the time I thought you were just going to walk in and close us down to punish my dad.'

'Despite what you may have heard I would *never* be that careless with people's jobs.' Forced to confront the depth of his own misjudgement, Damon felt a stab of guilt. 'I admit that my anger towards your father blinded business sense. I wasn't thinking clearly. I misjudged you, but you must admit that I had reason.'

'Because I was excluded from school?'

'Because nothing about Prince Advertising is professional.'

'Actually, you're wrong about that. We don't do things your way, but that isn't the same as being unprofessional.'

She paused to watch as a boat passed under the bridge, lights twinkling and music playing. On the deck, a couple were locked in a passionate embrace and suddenly Damon wished he hadn't agreed to a walk.

Everything made him think about that kiss in the hotel suite.

To distract himself, he kept the conversation focused on work.

'I can see that you have original ideas, but original ideas are no good if they're not supported by sound business practice. Money was leaking from your company. Do you have any idea how close you were to bankruptcy?'

She was still watching the couple kissing. 'Yes.'

'Is that why you all took a pay cut?'

'The board wanted redundancies. None of us wanted that. We're a team. We're happy working together. And we're good. I've known some of these people since I was a child and used to come to the office after school to help. The problems we face aren't anything to do with lack of talent. You're a clever man and you've looked at the numbers. You know that the money leaking from the company was pouring straight into the pockets of the board.'

'I understand that. It's the reason I fired them although at the time I didn't know just how bad they were. What I don't understand is why your father allowed it to happen. He should have had tighter control on what was going on.'

Even though it wasn't cold, she drew the coat more tightly around her. 'My father has always treated the company more as a hobby than a business. Sometimes he's interested and sometimes he isn't.' Her voice was deceptively light. 'He didn't keep a rein on the board and without him there they took more and more liberties. He stopped showing interest in the company altogether about six months ago—about the same time he started seeing your sister. He's been behaving like a teenager in love ever since. The board wanted cost savings.'

Damon kept his anger on a tight leash. 'And the obvious solution, apart from slashing their own spending, was redundancy.'

'My dad set up the company twenty-five years ago and some of the people who worked for him are still there. They're loyal, lovely people.' Her gaze flickered briefly to his. 'And before you say it, yes, I know that business can't run successfully on loyal, lovely people alone. We all figured that as long as we were still employed it could turn around so we agreed to the pay cut. I suppose we were all hoping for a miracle.' With a wry smile, she stroked a strand of blonde hair away from her face. 'And then my father and your sister went missing. And you showed up.'

Damon paused, unused to confiding in anyone but surprised to find that he wanted to. 'We had a row. Just over two weeks ago. Arianna told me she was in love with someone and that I was going to lose it when she told me who.' He pressed his fingers to the bridge of his nose, regretting that encounter. 'She was right. I did lose it.'

'I can imagine. We were never exactly your favourite family.'

His hand dropped slowly. 'You were right when you accused me of acting emotionally—I did. But it was like watching a train crash in slow motion—you can see disaster and you want to take charge and stop it happening.'

'Why do you feel you have to stop things happening?'

'That night we were told about our parents—I thought she was too young to understand. She wasn't.' The cold feeling spread through him and he had an urgent need to shake it off, to outrun it. 'She crawled onto my lap and sobbed and sobbed. Wouldn't let go. I have never felt more helpless and inadequate than I did that night. I promised myself I was never going to let her be hurt like that again.'

Polly matched her stride to his as they crossed the bridge and started to walk along the embankment towards the hotel. 'She was a child then. She's an adult now.'

'I'm more parent than brother and I don't think a parent ever stops feeling responsible.' It was typical, he thought, that a woman would want to unpeel that statement and look beneath the surface. He wondered what had possessed him to make such an unguarded comment when normally he kept his feelings tightly locked away. 'Let's get back to the hotel.'

'In other words you don't want to talk about it. Sorry. Shouldn't have asked.' She was light on her feet, sure-footed as she negotiated paving stones and cobbles. 'So what happens now? You took over the company thinking that you'd be able to influence my father. But my father doesn't care about the company at the moment. He's obsessed with your sister.' Her face was pale in the twinkling evening light and Damon watched her, realising that he'd given virtually no thought to how she felt about it all.

'It must have been hard for you, seeing him involved with women your age.'

Her tongue moistened her lower lip. 'School was hard. My father used to drive a soft-top sports car and the blonde in the front was as much of an accessory as the CD-player. If anything is designed to make you a target, it's having a parent who behaves like that.'

'Was that why you rebelled?'

She gave a funny crooked smile. 'I didn't rebel. I had a problem and I sorted it. It's what I've always done.'

'You had three boys in your bedroom—the bedroom you shared with my sister. How was that sorting a problem?'

'It happened ten years ago! I refuse to be continually judged on something I did ten years ago. Get over it.' She walked surprisingly quickly for someone quite petite and he cursed softly and followed, deciding that she was infinitely more complicated than he'd first thought.

He was getting the sense that he'd misjudged her yet again, and yet her misdemeanour had been witnessed by several members of staff so he knew that this time there was no mistake. What was there to misjudge? At fourteen years old she'd been caught in her underwear in her bedroom with three boys—an offence dealt with by exclusion.

They'd reached the hotel and she smiled at the doorman and greeted him in French.

Amazed that she managed to be chatty even in a foreign language, Damon extracted her from what promised to be a lengthy conversation and urged her forwards. 'So why is your title executive assistant when clearly you should be on the creative team? It's not a fair reflection of your responsibilities or your contribution.'

'Life isn't always fair, Mr Doukakis.' She walked into the apartment ahead of him, exchanging a cheerful greeting with his security team who Damon dismissed with a faint movement of his head.

'I think we should probably drop the formality, don't you?'

As the door closed behind the last security man she turned her head and something flickered in her eyes.

'Fine. Let's drop the formality.' There was a moment's hesitation and she drew in a long, slow breath, as if she were plucking up courage. Then, without shifting her gaze from his face, she lifted her chin and slowly, provocatively, undid the buttons of her coat and allowed it to slide to the floor. The jacket of her suit followed and his eyes slid to the thin black straps her camisole. All evening he'd had tantalising glimpses of sexy lace and now he saw that the whole thing was lace, the elaborate pattern exposing a suggestion of creamy skin.

His mouth dried. '*Theé mou*, what are you doing?'

'I'm dropping the formality. And my clothes, now that you mention it.' A slight smile tugging at the corners of her mouth, she walked towards him. 'What's the matter, Damon? Worried about that self-control of yours? Worried you won't be able to walk away from chemistry?' Her hand locked into the front of his shirt and she pulled him towards her, her thick lashes a tempting veil over eyes that glittered like jewels. Her lips parted and Damon felt his brain shut down.

He ought to push her away right now.

He ought to—

Her fingers locked behind his head and drew his head down and his mouth melded with warm, honeyed temptation. She tasted exquisite, the subtle stroke of her tongue against his bottom lip a hot, erotic fantasy, and he felt lust slam into him with shocking force. Resisting, he lifted his hands to push her away but instead found himself cupping her face, his fingers exploring the softness of her skin and the delicate lines of her jaw. If the kiss they'd shared earlier had been a full-on demonstration of the power of sexual attraction this was softer, more subtle. But it was no less devastating in its effect. Her sweet mouth seduced his with a slow, sure gentleness that ripped away his defences and sent fire tearing through every part of him.

Balancing on the dangerous knife-edge of a new addiction, he felt his power to control his emotions and actions drain at a frightening rate. The part of his brain warning him to stop this madness right now was eclipsed by the part that reached out greedily for the fulfilment of pleasure. A whisper of silk brushed his hand and he removed the clip in her hair and dropped it on the floor, allowing the river of softness to slide over her shoulders. With a husky groan he slid his fingers into that soft sheet of hair and deepened the kiss. The intense flame of sexual chemistry scorched both of them and this time when he gently stroked her face he discovered that his hand was shaking. Devoured by emotions he'd never felt before, he smoothed his palms over her shoulders, feeling nothing but a desperate urge to explore the rest of her. The thin spaghetti straps of her camisole surrendered to the pressure of his fingers and slid away, leaving no barrier between her flesh and his mouth. As he pressed his lips to her throat he heard her gasp, felt the rapid thrum of her pulse under his mouth

And then she stepped away.

Disorientated, unbalanced by her unexpected withdrawal, it took Damon a moment to absorb the fact that she'd retreated. He stretched out a hand to haul her back but she was already out of reach, those beautiful eyes unreadable as she slowly and deliberately slid the straps of her top back up to her shoulders.

His mind in lockdown, he struggled to speak. 'What are you doing?'

'I'm resisting chemistry. It's called self-discipline.' In a husky voice, she threw his words right back at him. 'You just have to say no. Isn't that right, Damon? Just because you're insanely good at kissing, that doesn't give you the right to make a fool of me. Don't *ever* do that again.' In a single graceful movement she retrieved her clothes and turned to walk towards the second bedroom. 'Sleep well.'

CHAPTER SEVEN

POLLY leaned over her private section of balcony, sucking in air and trying to lower her blood pressure. Her entire body screamed with frustration, and she didn't know whether to plunge under a cold shower or pull on her running shoes and pound the streets of Paris.

She dug her hands into her hair but that just reminded her of the moment he'd done the same thing so she folded her arms instead and paced backwards and forwards, breathing deeply.

Of all the stupid things to do.

What on earth had possessed her? She'd been running on adrenaline, on such a high after the success of her meeting with Gérard that she'd virtually danced along the streets of Paris. And, yes, it had felt *good* to witness the moment Damon had finally realised just what an enormous contribution she made to the company. But that didn't explain why she'd suddenly performed the equivalent of a pole dance in the middle of his hotel suite.

Wondering how on earth she was going to face him again, she covered her face with her hands. Perhaps it had been seeing all those lovers holding hands and kissing. Paris was a city for lovers. Romance. Or maybe it was just about pride.

All evening she'd been simmering, really angry that he'd made such a fool of her.

Her hands dropped and she swallowed hard.

In walking away from her earlier, he'd proved that he was

firmly in control. She'd wanted to hit back—to snap that control.

And she had.

But now she was the one paying the price.

Yes, she'd proved her point and walked away, but her body was on fire and the way she was feeling was driving her crazy. If this was how chemistry felt then no wonder people behaved stupidly.

'Polly—'

Hearing his rough voice, she whirled round and saw him standing there. His shirt gaped where she'd ripped at his buttons and his eyes were an intense, unfathomable black in a face taut with tension.

'Get out of here.' The words stuck to her dry mouth and she licked her lips, trying not to think about the way it felt to kiss him. Her own self-control was non-existent and she hated him for that. 'We're even.'

'Kissing me was your idea of punishment?'

'You kissed me to prove a point. I was doing the same thing.' Except that it had backfired. Disturbed by the look in his eyes, she a step backwards, terrified and fascinated in equal measure. 'You're the one who started this.'

'I know. I accept full responsibility—and you're right to be angry. It was a selfish, careless thing to do—' he slid his hand into her hair and cupped the back of her head, drawing her towards him '—and I apologise.' His soft words threw her because she hadn't thought him capable of apology any more than she'd thought him capable of gentleness. And that gentleness was all the more seductive because it came from a man for whom strength and self-assurance was the norm.

The intimacy of the moment wrapped itself around her like a thousand invisible strands drawing them together. It was a connection she didn't understand and therefore couldn't fight.

The whole of Paris was spread beneath them like a glittering magic carpet, the air scented by the flowers that tumbled from the pots that turned the terrace into an exotic rooftop garden. As a setting, it couldn't have been more romantic.

And she didn't want romantic.

She'd seen what 'romantic' did to people and suddenly she was terrified. Why the hell had she kissed him? After that first time she should have known that it was dangerous—stupid. He'd made her feel something she'd never felt and didn't want to feel.

'OK, you've said sorry and that's great—fine—now you can leave. Preferably right now because I can't breathe properly when you're standing this close.' She lifted her hand to his chest and encountered hard muscle and a man who clearly wasn't going to budge. 'Seriously, Damon, let's just forget the whole thing and—oh, God—' The sudden pressure of his mouth on hers silenced the rest of her sentence and she moaned indistinctly as his tongue swept into her mouth, the erotic invasion sending her head into a crazy spin and her senses into freefall. Sexual excitement flashed through her, ignited by the skill of his kiss and the sure strength of his hands on her body.

'Damon—' She moaned his name as he cupped her breast with his hand, the rough pad of his thumb grazing over her nipple. 'Honestly, we can't—' She gasped as he drew her against him and restraint and common sense melted in a warm puddle of molten desire. 'Or maybe we can.' Her arms were round his neck, pulling him down to her as he pulled her in. 'Just tell me quickly—are you about to walk away again?'

'No chance.' His hands were sure and bold as they slid down her back. 'Neither are you.'

'Good, because if you stop this time I just might have to kill you.'

Her hands were inside his shirt, her fingers sliding slowly

over warm male skin. His body was lean and muscled but that came as no surprise because she already knew he was strong. What surprised her was the complexity and depth, the emotions that flickered under the cool, controlled surface he presented to the world.

When she'd kissed him earlier, his guard had slipped. For a fleeting moment he'd lost his grip on that rigid control that characterised the way he lived his life. The fact that she was the one who'd slid under those defences intensified the excitement.

They kissed with a searing, primitive hunger that burned up logic and caution, their mouths greedy, seeking, hot as they feasted, lost in the burning fire of the moment. The world centred on the two of them. She was no longer aware of the city that stretched beneath her, or the warm whisper of the night breeze. All she was aware of was him—this man who kissed her as if he understood everything about who she was and what she needed.

She'd never understood how sex could drive people to make foolish decisions. Until now.

When he lifted her in an easy movement and carried her from her small terrace through to the master bedroom suite, she simply tightened her arms around his neck and kept on kissing him. Paris sparkled through the windows but neither of them spared the city a single glance.

As he lowered her gently to the centre of the enormous bed, she pushed his shirt off his shoulders and he shrugged it away. The swell of muscle in his shoulders bunched as he supported his weight and came down on top of her, the movement so innately masculine that her breath caught.

Even though part of her hated to admit it, the physical power of him was part of the attraction. Dark and handsome, he was unequivocally male, every touch and kiss assured and confident as he dragged her into a whole new world of dangerous desire.

As his warm, clever mouth trailed down her body Polly writhed against the silk sheets, her body gripped by such intense excitement that she couldn't keep still. The need to move her hips was almost painful and she writhed and shifted until she felt his strong hands grasp her, holding her captive. Deprived of the only means of easing the burning ache between her thighs, she gave a murmur of protest—a murmur that turned to a gasp as he spread her thighs and used his mouth on her, the skilled flick of his tongue driving her into a frenzy of desperation. It was impossibly intimate but she didn't even care, and she surrendered to the feeling, mindless to everything except the pleasure he created and controlled. The excitement built and spread until it exploded in a bright burst of light, her climax so extraordinarily intense that she couldn't breathe.

As consciousness gradually seeped back into her spinning head she opened her eyes, but she had no time to recover before he moved up her body and kissed her. Sensation after sensation slammed into her and she wondered dimly how it was possible to want someone this much. It was a devouring hunger, a greed she'd never before imagined, and this time she took control as she pushed at his chest and rolled. She was aware that he was far too strong to be pushed anywhere he didn't want to go but it was clear he was willing to play her game and he rolled onto his back, his eyes glittering dark as he watched her from under those thick black lashes.

As she kissed her way down his body she heard him groan and then mutter something in Greek, something she didn't understand but which told her he was as carried away by the moment as she was. Relishing her own power, she slid her mouth over the velvet length of him, using her tongue and her lips to drive him wild until he groaned and lifted her towards him.

'I want you. Now.'

In the grip of the same desperation, Polly moved up his body and straddled him. His need to be in control seemed to have left him and she positioned herself over him, her nerve-endings sizzling with awareness as she felt his swollen hardness brush against her. His eyes narrowed to two dangerous slits, he closed his hands around her hips and thrust upwards. Sure and confident, he drove into her and she gave a soft gasp at the feel of him as he surged deep. Just for a moment she thought *He's too big*, but then he paused, his fingers biting into her flesh as he held her where he wanted her.

'You're incredibly tight. Relax, *agape mou*—'

She couldn't relax. Her body was on fire, the power of his invasion momentarily shocking her out of the sexual trance that had held her in its grip.

His gaze sharpened and the beginnings of a frown touched his brow. '*Theé mou*, have you ever—?'

Polly cut his sentence off with her mouth, nibbling at his lips, stroking with her tongue, until the unspoken question turned into a kiss that blew away the unexpected tension. Shivering with longing, she lifted mouth from his so that she could look at him, her breathing rapid as she rocked her hips, taking him deep. This time as he surged into her he watched her, and that depth of connection increased the chemistry until she knew on some deep, subliminal level that this was so much more than just physical pleasure. It was the most erotic, intimate experience of her life. Sensation built and clawed at her until he drove them both over the edge and the explosion of ecstasy ripped through them both simultaneously. Wave after wave of it slammed into her until she collapsed against him, the only sound in the room the breath tearing at her throat.

She felt the pounding of his heart and then his arms tightened around her, his hand gently stroking the length of her spine. He didn't speak, but she knew he was as shocked as she was.

Lying there in the circle of his arms, Polly felt a surge of raw terror.

Oh, God, what had she done?

Not the sex—although she'd shocked herself and very probably she'd shocked Damon, too. No, what really terrified her was the intensity of emotion that had accompanied the physical. The connection, the closeness—they were the things she'd spent her life avoiding.

She lay for a minute, her head resting on the hard muscle of his chest, her thoughts private and her expression concealed.

The panic spread slowly. As deadly and insidious as smoke sneaking through a burning building, it seeped into every part of her.

She felt his hand still on her back and wondered what he was thinking.

He was bound to be regretting it, wasn't he? Damon Doukakis was a man who never lost control and he'd just lost control. And with a woman who aggravated him.

Trying to extricate herself from a hideous situation, Polly rolled away from him but a strong hand snaked out and caught her.

'Where do you think you're going?'

'To bed.'

'You're in bed.' His voice husky, he rolled her onto her back and slid his hand into her hair, forcing her to look at him. '*My* bed. What's the matter?'

She wanted to run but the weight of his body pinned her

to the bed, and as his mouth lowered to hers in a possessive kiss the desire to escape evaporated and she kissed him back, driven wild by the ruthless demands of his mouth.

'*Theé mou,* you are the hottest, sexiest woman I have ever met,' he groaned, sliding his hand under her bottom and lifting her against him. 'What the hell are you doing to me?

She felt the hunger in him, the feverish tension. Instinctively she knew he felt the same primitive chemistry that kept her trapped in the bed when she knew she should leave. The passion was raw and entirely mutual.

Wrapping her arms around his body, she looked up at him, her heart drumming against her chest in a crazy rhythm. The muscles in his shoulders were pumped up and hard and her stomach squirmed with liquid desire even as her brain rejected the image. 'Stop playing the dominant male.'

'I'm not playing at anything.' His voice thickened with lust he brought her hips into contact with the hard thrust of his arousal. 'And you want me as much as I want you.'

Oh, yes, she wanted him. She was every bit as desperate as he was. And the burning need overwhelmed the terror. 'I suppose I'll let you be the one in charge this time.' Lowering her eyelids, she teased him. 'It's only fair as I was the one in control last time.'

Teasing her right back, he gave a slow, dangerous smile and lowered his mouth to hers, murmuring words against her lips. 'I hate to break this to you, but you weren't the one in control, *agape mou.*'

'I had you on your back.'

'I was on my back, that's true—' his eyes darkened and he tightened his hand on her bottom, lifting her '—but only because that's where I chose to be. I had you exactly where I wanted you.' Shifting her position subtly, he surged into her, and Polly gave a sob as she felt him filling her, the silken force of him stretching her sensitised flesh and fusing the two of them together.

For a moment he paused, letting her feel what he did to her, and she dug her nails into the satin-smooth skin of his back as she struggled with the fire that consumed her.

With a groan he withdrew slightly and then surged into her again. 'You feel so good…' With every driving thrust he sent the excitement tighter and tighter until release came in a shattering explosion of sweet sensation, the experience so sublime, so perfect, that she felt it in every corner of her trembling frame.

Slowly, the excitement faded to pleasure and then to a soft hum of blissful contentment.

For a moment she just lay there, slightly dazed.

And then the terror returned.

Emerging from a sex-induced coma, Damon woke to find himself alone in the bed.

As the morning light poured into the bedroom, it took him a moment to orientate himself. Turning his head slowly, he eyed the tangled sheets and found himself struggling with emotions entirely foreign to him.

He'd spent a wild night with Polly Prince.

Covering his eyes with his forearm, he swore long and fluently. It didn't help to acknowledge that it had started with him trying to prove his ability to control his decisions and actions.

Control?

Where had control been during their marathon sex session? The irony slapped him in the face. In trying to prove control, he'd disproved it. And he'd done it again and again, until she'd been limp and pliant and had finally fallen asleep on his shoulder, those incredible limbs wrapped around him.

Just thinking about it made him hard again and he gave an

exclamation of frustration and sprang from the bed, trying to dispel the image of a smouldering Polly letting her coat slip to the floor.

That whole striptease had been his undoing.

Striding into the bathroom, he stepped into the shower, hoping that a blast of freezing water would cool his body and his brain.

He needed to stop feeling and *think*.

As if his life wasn't already complicated enough, he'd now complicated it still further. It wasn't just the situation between his sister and her father, or even the fact that she now worked for him and he made a point of never becoming involved with an employee. No, the real complication was that he didn't want a serious relationship. There was no way he wanted to be responsible for yet another human being's happiness. It was enough to have the burden of thousands of employees and one wayward sister. He didn't need anyone else added into the mix.

Damon turned the jets of the shower to full blast, knowing that the only way to deal with the situation was to be blunt. Honest.

The question was whether it was better to do it immediately, and risk subjecting himself to the company of an emotional female for the journey home, or whether to delay that conversation until they reached London and he could extricate himself from the fall-out with greater ease.

It was going to make it impossible to work with her, and it was clear to him that, despite his previous thoughts, she was a key player in the business. He suspected that Gérard's devotion to her was as much due to her creative imagination as her long legs.

Postponing the moment when he had to shatter Polly's romantic illusions, he shaved, dressed and dealt with his urgent calls. By the time he'd returned calls to people in London and Athens there was still no sign of her.

After the intimacies they'd shared the night before, he was surprised.

His jaw tightened and he tried to free himself of the uncomfortable suspicion that she'd been a virgin. Twenty-four-year-old virgins didn't exist, did they? Especially not virgins who seduced a man with a striptease and then proceeded to indulge in hot, steamy sex without a single blush or bat of an eyelash.

Dismissing the thought, he strode through the apartment in search of her.

Theé mou, he wasn't a man who avoided awkward situations. He just did what needed to be done, so why was he dragging his feet?

Even though he reminded himself that she'd been a more than willing partner, he still felt a sense of responsibility. He'd started it, hadn't he? By kissing her.

It was time to put an end to something he never should have started.

He found her seated on the balcony, talking to someone on the phone while she plugged numbers into a spreadsheet on her laptop.

Damon studied her face for evidence of distress but she looked animated and energised as she negotiated a price with someone on the end of the phone.

When she finally ended the call she was so absorbed in the work she was doing she didn't immediately notice him. Looking at her now, he wondered how he could ever have accused her of being lazy. It was obvious she'd been working for hours.

'Don't you ever sleep?'

She glanced up then, her cheeks dimpling into a warm

smile. 'You're a fine one to talk. I hear your average working day is twenty hours.'

'I'm the boss.'

'So you're setting an example? Never mind that. I'm glad you're here because I really need to talk to you.' She hit 'save' and Damon drew in a breath, bracing himself for the inevitable conversation.

She looked so happy. Lit up inside.

It was obvious she'd succumbed to that dizzy, crazy feeling that came at the beginning of a new relationship.

No doubt she was plotting out their future as women always did. And he was about to take those plans and shatter them. *This* was why he avoided responsibilities. He never forgot that the fear of letting down the people close to him was what had driven his father over the edge of despair.

Sweat broke out on the back of his neck. 'Polly—'

'Can you take a quick look at this?' She turned the laptop so that he could see the screen. Her hair was pinned haphazardly on top of her head and she was wearing a dress in a wild shade of purple. Her pink notebook lay face-down on the table. 'I've prepared two proposals—one for a massive budget and one for a shockingly massive budget.' She gave a wicked smile. 'I'm hoping that Gérard will be so impressed by the ideas he won't look at how much they're costing. What do you think? You know him better than me—if you think I've gone over the top then just say so. I suddenly decided that we might be able to do something in Fashion Week so I've made a few calls.'

Her focus on work threw him. 'You want me to look at the budget? That's what you wanted to talk about?'

'Yes.' Her eyes were back on the screen as she reached for the glass of water she'd placed on the table. 'Ideally I'd like to e-mail this today while he's still excited about everything we discussed. I don't want him to back down on that figure he mentioned last night. If this piece of business is going to be worth that much to the company, there's no way you'll have to make the staff redundant.'

Braced for an entirely different conversation, Damon couldn't focus. 'I'll take a look at your proposal later.'

'Do you think you could do it now? When I get back to the office I want to be able to gather the team together and give them a morale-boosting talk. I thought after last night you'd find it impossible to justify doing something so mean as letting anyone go.'

'After last night?' He repeated her words, shocked by the raw emotion that rushed through him. 'You think the fact that we had sex will affect my business decisions?'

Her jaw dropped. 'I was talking about the meeting with Gérard.'

Of course. The meeting. Damon pressed his fingers to the bridge of his nose, realising that he was in serious trouble. 'We are having two different conversations here.'

'I think we must be.' She looked genuinely astonished. 'I'm having a conversation about the staff. I can't concentrate on anything or enjoy my work when I'm watching my back and worrying about job losses. I just want that sorted. What are you having a conversation about?'

His eyes dropped to her mouth and his body tightened as he remembered how she tasted. The fact that she was thinking about her staff and not the night they'd spent threw him. Normally after a night of steamy sex women wanted to know what was going to happen next. They went into full planning mode. Polly appeared to have skipped that ritual and was just making the assumption that they were already a couple.

'You're very chirpy for someone who had virtually no sleep,' he said cautiously. 'I thought you weren't a morning person.'

'I didn't think I was either.' She leaned forward and changed a figure on the spreadsheet. 'But apparently a night of crazy sex does wonders to wake me up. I wish I'd known sooner. I would have done it years ago. It's probably better for you than strong coffee.'

Digesting the implication of those words, Damon breathed deeply. 'So it *was* your first time.' Her confession intensified the suffocating feeling that had begun from the moment he'd woken up. 'Polly '

'It's hard for me to work out how to staff this account until I know what your plans are.'

'*Theé mou*, will you *stop* talking about work?'

Startled, she looked up at him. 'Sorry, but this account is really important. It's worth loads to the company...' Her voice trailed off as she looked at his face. 'You're behaving really weirdly, if you don't mind me saying. Just a couple of days ago you were telling me to take my lazy self and do some work and now you're telling me to stop thinking about work. It's very confusing.'

She couldn't possibly be more confused than him. 'I was wrong to say that. I was wrong about *you*,' Damon breathed. 'I've already apologised, but I apologise again.'

'Well, I was pretty wrong about you, too. I thought you were a demented workaholic with an unhealthy focus on the bottom line. But right now, when I *really* need you to talk about work, you seem incapable of focusing. It's very frustrating.'

'Why were you a virgin?'

'What sort of a question is that?!' Her face turned scarlet. 'Because no man ever wanted to take me to bed before, I suppose. Thanks for pointing that out. And now can we end this conversation? I don't know much about morning-after etiquette but I'm pretty sure that embarrassing your partner isn't on the list.'

'You were excluded from school at fourteen because you had three boys in your room,' he said thickly. 'So we both know you're not some blushing innocent.' The error in his thinking blazed in front of his eyes. She might not have been blushing, but she *had* been innocent. He'd suspected it at the time but he'd been too carried away by the whole erotic experience to act on that suspicion. 'What the hell transformed you from vamp to virgin?'

'I never said I was a vamp. You made that assumption. Along with a few others.'

'I made that assumption based on the evidence.'

'Mmm. Good job you're not a lawyer.' She gave a tiny shrug and fiddled with her pen. 'So—Arianna obviously never talked to you about that episode?'

The tension was like a layer of steel in his back. 'I didn't ask for details. I decided it was safer to put the whole thing behind us.'

'Right. Probably wise.'

Exasperation rose in him. 'I remember that day very clearly and you didn't make a single excuse. You just stood there with a defiant look on your face and let them throw you out of the school. Permanently. Not *once* did you defend yourself or try and stop it happening.'

'I didn't want to stop it happening.'

Far beneath them the sound of horns blared as the impatient French negotiated the Paris traffic but Damon was oblivious. 'You *wanted* to be excluded?'

'Yes. That was the plan.'

'Plan?' He breathed slowly. 'You're telling me that you engineered the whole thing so that you'd be asked to leave the school? Why would you want that?'

'Because I was being bullied. Badly bullied.' Her tone was matter-of-fact. 'I tried other ways to sort it out but none of them worked. So I decided I had to leave the school.'

'*You* decided—?' Digesting the implications of the statement, Damon struggled to focus. 'And your father didn't have anything to say about that?'

'I didn't ask him. It was my problem. I sorted it.'

'If I have a problem, I'm expected to sort it out myself.'

'Did you talk to the teachers?'

'Yes.' She looked at him as if he were clearly stupid. 'They spoke to the bullies, who were so angry that I'd told on them they set fire to my hair. Fortunately Arianna walked into the room and we managed to put it out, which was a relief because burnt hair is *not* a good look.'

Damon gritted his teeth. 'What happened then?'

'We trimmed the ends. It was fine. It actually suited me shorter.'

'Not your hair, the bullying. Why didn't you tell your father?'

'Why would I tell my father?'

'Well, because—' Damon found himself at a loss for words. 'You were fourteen years old. It was his responsibility to come down to the school and sort it out.'

'That isn't his style. He prefers me to sort things out myself and that's fine with me. I'm grateful to him. I'm quite independent as a result of it. But I did feel guilty that Arianna got drawn into the whole episode.'

'So you didn't invite the boys to your room because you wanted to party?'

'No. I paid them to come and hang out while I danced in my underwear with a bottle of whisky in my hand. Someone tipped off the head teacher who promptly caught me. Which was as we'd planned, obviously. I thought it was an extremely creative solution. Anyway, it did the trick and the boys didn't seem to mind helping us out.'

Mind? Damon tried to obliterate the image of Polly writhing in her underwear with the express purpose of getting herself thrown out of school. 'Why did the other girls bully you?'

She wrinkled her nose. 'Mostly because of my dad, I suppose. As I said to you last night, it was social suicide having a parent turning up in a sports car with a young blonde in the front seat. I suppose if it hadn't been that it probably would have been something else. They just pick on whatever suits them—red hair, glasses, fat thighs—you know what bullies are like.'

He didn't, but she obviously did. 'What about your next school.'

'Oh, that worked out really well. I picked a nice day school close to my house.'

'*You* picked it?'

'Yes. I went to see a couple and chose one that did a lot of art and creative stuff. I thought it would suit me perfectly.'

'You—' Damon broke off, unable to believe what he was hearing. 'You're saying that you picked the school by yourself? That your father didn't go with you?'

'Why would he? I got myself kicked out of school. It was my job to find myself another one, which turned out great,' she added cheerfully. 'I don't see why you're so shocked about the whole thing.'

'Bullying is unacceptable behaviour. You should have had support. You shouldn't have had to leave.'

'Leaving was the best thing that happened to me. I hated that school and so did Arianna.'

'*Arianna* hated it?'

'Yes. The girls were vile. Honestly, I think we were just unlucky with our year group or something. She didn't really want to hang around there without me and she thought my party plan would work better if she joined in.'

The news that his sister had also hated the school was a solid blow deep in his gut. Shaken by those unexpected revelations, Damon turned the full force of his own guilt into anger. 'Why the hell didn't one of you tell me the truth?'

'Arianna did say that she might, but you were storming and ranting and looking like thunder so I think she lost her nerve. Look—just forget it. It's such a long time ago I can hardly remember.'

He didn't believe her for a moment. It had obviously left deep, permanent scars. 'Don't lie. For once, I want the truth.'

'The truth is that it doesn't matter any more. None of it. I've moved on.' She was silent for a moment, as if her own words had come as a surprise to her. Then a tiny smile touched the corners of her mouth and she sat back in her chair, as if she were surprised by something. 'Wow. I've said those words a million times and never really meant them. But this time I really mean them! I really *have* moved on.' Her smile widening, she sprang to her feet and did an impromptu twirl. Then she grabbed the front of his coat and her eyes shone into his. 'Do you have any idea how good that feels? You can deal with something, you can put it behind you, but that's not the same as actually being over it. And I'm *over* it! Honestly, truly over it.'

Observing this unrestrained display of ecstasy with growing bemusement, Damon found himself overwhelmed by a sudden urge to drag her back to bed. Staring down at the tiny dimple at the corner of her mouth, he wondered what had happened to restraint and discipline.

'I can see now what a difficult time you've had.' The words stuck in his throat. 'And then I took over your father's company and stormed and ranted and looked like thunder.' *And made things worse for her.*

And he was about to make them worse still by telling her that their relationship was over. That whatever they'd shared was just a one off, never to be repeated.

'You were worried about your sister. I get that. Don't worry.' Still smiling, she stretched her arms above her head and yawned. 'Arianna is lucky to have you. You might be misguided sometimes, but I know you care. That's the thing that matters.'

Damon dragged his eyes from her slender arms and tried to wipe the memories of her sliding those arms around his neck. 'Misguided?'

'Well, you smother her, which means she always feels the need to rebel. But don't worry about it. Plenty of parents make that mistake and you're not even her parent.' There was a flash of admiration in her gaze. 'I don't know how you did it. None of the sixteen-year-old-boys I've met are capable of caring for themselves, let alone someone else. My dad, who was several decades older than you, completely freaked out when my mum walked out on him and left me with him. Not that I remember because I was only two. But I remember us both having a laugh about it one day. He told me that he sat there looking at me, and apparently I sat there looking at him. I didn't quite have to change my own nappy, but I learned pretty early on that if I wanted something done I had to do it myself. And I did things for him too.'

Damon was appalled at her parents' utterly selfish behaviour. 'How long was it until your father remarried the first time?'

'It felt like about five minutes. My dad is rubbish at being on his own. As soon as a relationship breaks down he latches onto the next person. I didn't even think much of it until I went to senior school—' She gave a matter-of-fact shrug. 'Everything is so much more complicated at senior school. Younger children are much more accepting of differences.'

Examining his own behaviour, and not liking what he saw, Damon paced to the balcony and stared down at the Paris streets, jammed with traffic. 'You are a very bright, very clever young woman. Why didn't you go to university?'

His question was met with silence and when he turned his head to look at her she gave what could only be described as a forced smile.

'I spent my childhood in and out of the company. The people were like my family. Once I started at the day school I often hung out there because it was more fun than going home to an empty house. I used to help Doris Cooper in the post room and then I'd find an empty desk somewhere and Mr Foster in Accounts used to help me with my maths homework. By the time I reached eighteen I could see the company was a mess. I could also see a way I could make a huge contribution and pay back some of their kindness to me. They were always worried that they'd lose their jobs. I didn't want that to happen.'

'My sources tell me your Mr Foster is struggling.'

'Because the board never invested in training.' She defended her colleague hotly. 'He just needs help with spreadsheets. I've been doing my best to train him because frankly he's the reason I did well at maths, but there isn't a whole lot of time in the day.'

'I imagine there isn't when you're running an entire company single-handed.' His dry tone earned him a frown.

'Don't mock me.'

'I'm not mocking you.'

'If I was responsible for the company then I didn't do a good job, did I?' she said in a gloomy voice. 'Because everyone could still be made redundant.'

'*Theé mou*, if I give you my assurance no one will be made redundant can we talk about something other than work for five minutes?!' Damon jabbed his fingers into his hair and wondered how the conversation he'd been planning had somehow been so dramatically derailed. Somehow what he had to say felt even harder in the light of what she'd just revealed. 'Polly—' with a huge effort, he controlled the tone of his voice '—we have to talk about what happens next.'

'Well, if you're serious about not making anyone redundant then I'll get straight on the phone to reassure everyone and—'

'Polly!' His tone finally snagged her attention.

'What? You're not about to tell me you were joking, are you?' Her face lost colour. 'Because that would be a really cruel thing to do.'

'I'm not joking. Everyone who previously worked for your father can keep their jobs.'

'Really?' Her expression was transformed from worry to wonderment and she flung her arms around him, dancing on the spot and hugging at the same time. 'Oh, thank you, thank you, I take back every evil thing I ever said about you.'

Easing her away from him before he found himself repeating his mistakes of the previous night, Damon realised that her cheeks were wet. 'Why are you crying?'

'I'm just so happy! You have no idea—' She covered her face with her hands and drew in a juddering breath. 'I knew what a mess everything was but I just didn't know how to sort it out.' She wiped her cheeks on her sleeve. 'Sorry. But those people have been part of my life since I was small.'

A small, lonely little girl whose father had no time for her, finding friends and comfort among the people he worked with. Shaken by a depth of emotion he hadn't felt before, Damon instinctively withdrew. 'If you could stop crying, that would be good.'

'Sorry.' She produced a tissue and blew her nose hard. 'I expect you're used to mopping up tears from all those women you make cry.'

'I do *not* make women cry.'

'Of course you do, but don't worry about it. Today you're

my hero. You can do no wrong. Thank you *so* much. Can we fly straight back to London now? I want to tell everyone.' Her nose was pink and her eyes glistened with tears and *still* she'd made no reference to what had happened between them.

He wondered whether she'd already mentally moved her things into his penthouse?

'Polly, we have to talk about what happened last night.'

No longer looking at him, she pushed the tissue into her pocket. 'What is there to talk about? We both know what happened, but honestly there's nothing to talk about as far as I'm concerned.'

Damon, who recognised evasive action when he saw it, refused to be deflected. 'So that's it? We have hot sex all night and you don't intend to mention it again?'

'Basically, yes. I'd rather no one knew, obviously, because I don't want all those nudges and winks, but I'm fairly sure you don't want that either, so I'm not worried that you'll say anything. Just forget it.'

She expected him to forget it? 'Polly—'

'Last night you kissed me to prove a point. I kissed you back to prove a point. It got a bit out of control.'

'Are you saying you didn't know what you were doing?'

'Of course I knew what I was doing! I wasn't drunk or anything.' She gave a tiny shrug. 'I don't understand the post mortem. So we had sex? This is the twenty-first century. No one is involved except us. We used protection. What's the problem?'

'You'd never had sex before.'

'Well, there's a first time for everything.' Her BlackBerry buzzed and she picked it up and opened an e-mail. 'I've never visited Paris before either, so it's been a time of firsts. What time are we flying home?'

Shocked by her matter-of-fact response to the situation,

Damon failed to process that question. 'So you have no intention of repeating the experience?'

'Visiting Paris?'

He ground his teeth. 'Sex.'

'Some time, probably.' Gathering up her notebook and pen, she stuffed them into her bag.

Goaded by her indifference, Damon shot out a hand and yanked her against him. 'Are you pretending you didn't feel anything?'

'No, of course not. What is the matter with you?'

'We spent seven hours having sex last night.'

'You don't have to tell me that. I was there.'

'Generally women want to talk about it afterwards,' he said silkily, '*not* walk away.'

She was silent for a moment and then she lifted her gaze to his. 'You're telling me that after sex you like to lie there and talk about it? Sorry, but I find that incredibly hard to believe. You strike me more as the get-her-out-of-my-bed-before-she-grows-roots-type.'

Damon inhaled sharply, because that assessment was startlingly close to the truth, and Polly gave a faint smile.

'See? I'm right again. And that's fine. You don't have to exhaust yourself trying to let me down tactfully. As far as I'm concerned, it's forgotten.'

The fact that she was proposing forgetting something so incredible irritated him as much as the thought of her prolonging their relationship had aggravated him just moments earlier.

The knowledge that he was behaving illogically simply fuelled his frustration. 'You want to forget it?'

'Yes, of course! You must have gathered by now that I'm rubbish at relationships. And you're obviously not exactly brilliant either. So that's fine. We're cool! I'm going to pack while you read my proposal.' With a reassuring smile, she disengaged herself, scooped up her laptop and strolled across the terrace towards the door that led to the second bedroom. 'I'm so thrilled you're not going to make people redundant. I feel really happy.'

Speechless, Damon stared after her.

She was happy because he wasn't going to make her colleagues redundant, not because they'd spent the night having mind-blowing, intimate sex.

She wanted to forget it had happened. There had been no awkward conversation, no full-scale demolition of inflated expectations. Apparently she didn't have any expectations. As far as she was concerned it had been a one-night stand.

This was his definition of a fairy tale ending and he waited to feel a rush of relief.

Nothing happened.

CHAPTER EIGHT

'THE budget is how much?' Debbie plopped down on the chair and fanned herself with her hand. 'That's incredible. You're a genius.'

'Gérard liked my ideas.'

'And Demon Damon can't fail to be impressed. I hope he comes crawling back with an apology.'

Careful not to look up, Polly scrolled through her 'to do' list. 'He isn't really Demon Damon. He's pretty decent, really. He just cares about his sister.' When Debbie didn't respond, Polly lifted her head. 'What?'

'Sorry, but isn't this rather an abrupt turnaround? Just two weeks ago he was the Big Bad Wolf poised to eat everyone in one gulp.'

Polly felt the fire burn in her cheeks and quickly turned back to her desk. 'He's guaranteed everyone's jobs. That wins my vote.'

'Mmm… So are you ever going to tell me what really happened in Paris? It's been two weeks and you've said virtually nothing.'

'I told you it was a very successful business meeting.'

'Obviously. But I wasn't talking about the meeting.'

'The Eiffel Tower looked pretty at night.'

'All right—let's stop messing around here and get straight to the point.' Debbie folded her arms and strolled round the desk so that she could see Polly's face. *Did he kiss you?*'

Polly felt the breath catch in her lungs. For two weeks she'd been trying not to think about Paris. And she'd tried especially hard not to think about the way Damon kissed. 'Will you leave it alone? What is the matter with you?'

'Oh, my God, he *did* kiss you.'

'Did you feed Romeo and Juliet while I was away?'

'You think I've put them on a diet?'

'Polly, I've just managed to agree a fantastic rate for those primetime ad slots.' Kim came scurrying across the office, the baby tucked against her shoulder and her BlackBerry in her other hand. 'I've sent you an e-mail.'

Relieved to be rescued from Debbie, Polly stretched out her arms and took the baby for a cuddle. 'I gather your child minder has let you down again? I can't believe how much he's grown in just two weeks.'

'Sorry I had to bring him in. I would have worked from home but I have to finish those magazine tie-ins for the *Run, Breathe, Live* campaign. Sam doesn't mind.'

Polly kissed Sam's downy head. 'Maybe not, but I have a feeling that the boss might. We have to introduce him to these things gradually or he'll have a heart attack. The plants and the fish almost finished him off. If he sees that you've brought Sam to work I think it might test his new found patience.'

'He isn't going to see. Damon flew to New York two weeks ago and hasn't been seen since.'

New York?

Falling on that crumb of news like a starving bird, Polly wanted to ask how Kim knew but she could see Debbie's foot tapping impatiently as she waited to be able to continue her interrogation. It would be asking for trouble to show too much interest in Damon's whereabouts.

She wished she'd known he wasn't even in the country.

Apparently she hadn't needed to spend the past two weeks watching the door in case he walked in.

'Maybe he *was* in New York,' Debbie murmured, 'but he's

not now. He just walked through the door. And you are holding
a baby.'

Polly's heart pounded against her chest and she knew she
was blushing. 'OK, this is *not* good. Why did he have to pick
this particular moment to check on us? Kim, take Sam into
one of the meeting rooms quickly. When Damon has gone,
we'll come and get you. Move.' She gave the baby back to
Kim and went to head Damon off.

Underneath the panic, she felt absurdly excited at the prospect of seeing him and that feeling horrified her. She was like
a puppy, wagging its tail. As she walked up to him all she
wanted to do was fling her arms round his neck. 'Hi there.
Good trip? Did you hear back from Gérard? He called me
this morning. Great news.' She tried to urge him back towards
the door and away from Kim and the baby, but he stood fast,
clearly happy to conduct the conversation in the middle of the
office.

'He rang me five minutes ago. Congratulations. I gather
he accepted your—how did you describe it?—"shockingly
massive" budget'. And he wants to talk to us about pitching
for more of their brands. Congratulations. You just landed
the biggest marketing fish in the pond. The only stipulation
is that he wants you to lead the team.' His eyes were dark.
Unfathomable. 'With that in mind I thought it was time to
discuss your position in the company. I don't think we can
have an executive assistant advising a vice president.'

'You'd better make me president, then. Then I can boss
you around.' Not for anything was she going to reveal how
pleased she was to see him again. She was about to ask him
more about his call with Gérard when a faint cry came from
the other side of the office. Polly froze in horror. 'So what position were you thinking of?' She raised her voice. 'Whatever
you think is fine by me.'

Damon flinched. 'Why are you shouting?'

'Because I'm really, really excited. I'm excited that Gérard went with the bigger programme.' Behind her she could hear the baby's muffled yells and sweat broke out on the back of her neck. 'Could we discuss it in your office? I really think this conversation is something we should have in private.'

'You want to go somewhere more private?'

Realising that she was now trapped into the position of having to be alone with him, Polly felt her heart-rate double. But what choice did she have? She didn't want him finding out that Kim had brought her baby into the office. He'd go into meltdown. 'Absolutely. There are some things that should be confidential.' Without giving him a chance to respond, she strode towards the stairs furthest from the crying baby.

When she realised that he was following her, she sighed with relief.

As they reached his office, she smiled at his personal assistant. 'Hi, Janey, your plants are looking lovely.'

'They do cheer the place up. Thanks for the recommendations. Can I bring you coffee, Mr Doukakis?'

Damon was staring at the plants in disbelief. 'Where did those come from?'

'I ordered them and they just arrived.' Janey smiled calmly. 'I admired the ones on Polly's floor and she advised me on which to buy. The plants need to be quite tolerant.'

'I know the feeling,' Damon breathed, and Polly grinned and nudged him towards the office.

'A few little plants aren't going to destroy your mega-efficient office atmosphere. Relax.'

'Polly, that plant was at least six foot. Not by anyone's standards could it be described as "little".'

'They create a very healthy working environment.'

'Next you will be asking me to provide fish as standard office equipment.'

'No, I don't think so.' Polly wondered whether he was

finding the conversation as hard as she was. They were talking about plants and fish but what she really wanted to say was *Why are you back?* and *Did you miss me?* 'Fish are very different. They need very specific care. They wouldn't be any good for people who aren't interested.'

'I was being ironic.'

'I know, but you take yourself far too seriously so I thought I'd play along. The plants aren't going to hurt you, Damon. They're not flesh-eating ones. Now, about this promotion—' Trying not to look at the width of his shoulders or the sexy curve of his mouth, she flopped down in the chair next to his desk. 'I hope I'm going to get a huge glass office and lots of fawning secretaries?'

'You'd be miserable in an office. You have to be surrounded by people and noise to function.'

The fact that he was starting to understand her so well was more than a little unsettling. 'OK, so no office and no fawning secretaries. You wanted to talk about my job?'

'I've been thinking about how best to use your skills. You seem to have been doing everything single-handed. You're undoubtedly creative, but you're also an organiser so I don't want to limit you.' He sprawled in the chair on the other side of his desk, watching her through those eyes that could make a woman's pulse rate accelerate like a racehorse at the finish line.

Remembering how he'd looked when he'd made love to her, Polly shifted in her chair and tried to concentrate. 'Whatever you think is fine by me. I'm really not that into titles and that sort of thing. I'm happy just doing the job.' She wished he'd stop looking at her as if he were contemplating pouncing from across the table.

Now that she was in front of him she couldn't stop thinking about sex, and she had a feeling he was having the same problem.

'You need to be client-facing, because you clearly have a gift for communication. So I propose to make you an account director, with full responsibility for the High Kick Hosiery account. Any creative work can be farmed out to my in-house team, but you can join them whenever they're brainstorming for new brands. And it's time you earned a decent salary.' He named a figure that made Polly feel faint.

'Gosh. That's a lot.'

'It's slightly above market rate,' he drawled. 'I never lose anyone for money.'

'Right. Well, that's great. But you're not going to lose me.' The moment he said the words she realised how they could be interpreted. 'At work, I mean. Obviously.'

A frown touched his dark brows, as if she'd said something that hadn't occurred to him before. 'I also wanted you to take a look at this.' He pushed a file across his desk. 'I thought you might be interested.'

Puzzled, Polly opened the file cautiously. Inside were materials on an MBA course. For a moment she couldn't breathe. Her hands shaking, she flicked through the pages. 'I—I sent off for this—'

'Every year for the past four years. I know. They told me when I requested the information.'

'Y-you spoke to them?'

'I wanted to be sure they'd take you if you wanted to go.'

'You're asking if I want to do an MBA?' Delight mingled with consternation. 'You don't want me to work for you any more?'

'I just said I don't want to lose you. You'd be doing both— working and studying. This way you still work for me and take time off when you need it.'

There was a loud buzzing in her ears. 'You're saying I could study *and* carry on at DMG?'

'It would be hard work. You might want to refuse.'

'Why? Because I'm generally lazy?' She kept it light to try and stifle the lump in her throat that had come from nowhere. He knew how badly she wanted a formal business qualification. He'd taken the time to research courses for her. 'I don't have a first degree.'

'They'd take into account your experience working in the business. You might have to take a couple of exams in order to qualify.'

It felt too good to be true. 'I wouldn't be able to afford it.'

'The company would pay. We'd be the beneficiaries of all that expertise.'

The lump in her throat grew. 'Why? Why would you do this for me?'

'If you're going to be working here long term and embarking on a proper career path with DMG then it's right that you should have a career plan.'

Polly didn't know whether to laugh or sob. 'I always thought you were a traditional Greek male. A woman's place is barefoot and pregnant in the kitchen and all that.'

'I am traditional. I have no problem with a woman being pregnant and barefoot in the kitchen if that's where she wants to be. But I'm also an astute businessman. I employ the best person for the job. I want you in my company. I'm happy to have you as you are, but you've always wanted to do this and I believe that if there's something you really want to do you should do it.'

Afraid she really was going to cry, Polly stood up quickly, clutching the file like a lifebelt. 'If it's OK with you I'm going to take this away and read it.'

'Sit down. I haven't finished.'

Polly sat, still overwhelmed by what he was offering.

He was silent for a moment, his long fingers tapping a

rhythm on his desk as he watched her. 'You and I are going out tonight.'

'Oh?' She tried to concentrate and behave professionally. 'We have a business dinner?'

'Not business. A date. You can leave your notebook behind.'

Date? Suddenly Polly forgot the file in her hand. 'You—you're asking me out?'

'Yes.'

Her heart pounded. 'I work for you.'

'I don't care,' he said testily. 'For once I'm going to do what I want to do just because I want to do it.'

'Oh.' If she'd thought she was happy before it was nothing to how she felt now, as her eyes met his. 'So—not for business or anything? Just for the hell of it?'

He gave a wry smile. 'Just for the sheer hell of it. You're always telling me I take myself too seriously.'

'Well—wow.'

'Does "wow" mean yes?'

She was grinning like an idiot, ridiculously pleased. 'Yes. Where are we going?'

'Somewhere special.'

'Ah, so no flamingo-pink tights.'

'You'll be dancing. I'll pick you up at ten.'

'Dancing?' Polly stood up again and this time she virtually floated towards the door, her mind already occupied by what she was going to wear.

'Oh and Polly—' his deep sexy drawl stopped her as she reached the door '—about the baby you're hiding in the office—'

Polly froze. 'Baby?' Her voice was a squeak. 'Er—what baby?'

'I don't want to give Health and Safety a heart attack so you can tell Kim we're looking into providing crèche facilities so that she can give the boot to that unreliable child-minder of hers.'

Polly clutched the door. 'How do you know about Kim's problem with the baby?'

'He was in your offices the day I came in and fired the board.'

'You *knew* the baby was in the office? And you didn't say anything?'

'There's a limit to how much disaster a man can absorb in one session. I'm told Kim is excellent at what she does so I'm going to use her in my media department. She needs good childcare.'

Polly gaped at him. 'Are you feeling all right?'

'Never better. Why?'

'Because you're being worryingly reasonable. A couple of weeks ago you would have fired the lot of us for bringing a baby into the office.'

'Kim is extremely productive and that to fire her would jeopardise the accounts you've won. On top of that, I know when I'm beaten.'

But he didn't look beaten. He looked sleek and in control. Far more in control than she was. She was fast discovering that it was possible to feel terrified, elated and panicky all at the same time.

'That's—great. Thanks. We have quite a few mothers on the team and childcare is always a nightmare.'

'So I understand. I'll fix it. And while we're at it you can stop giving Mr Foster lessons in spreadsheets. He's going on a proper training course starting tomorrow. Now, go. And don't buy my PA any more plants. The place is turning into a bloody jungle.'

'It's hard getting ready for an evening when you don't know where you're going.' Polly kept her coat tucked round her as she slid into the back seat of his chauffeur-driven car. 'What if I'm wearing the wrong thing?' She was hyper-aware of him—of his arm stretched across the back of the seat and the proximity of his thigh to hers.

He eyed her coat with one eyebrow raised. 'Take your coat off and I'll tell you.'

'I'm wearing the coat so that you can't tell me I'm wearing the wrong thing. You have a habit of freaking out over my clothes choice so I decided it was safer not to show you until we arrive. I don't want you to dent my confidence.'

'Fine, but promise me you are wearing *something* under the coat.'

'Sort of.'

With a groan and a sexy smile, he leaned his head back against the seat. 'I have a feeling I should have made you dinner in the apartment instead of taking you out in public.' He hesitated a moment and then closed his hand over hers, his fingers warm and strong.

Suddenly her insides felt jittery. She wanted to ask what tonight was all about.

Her impression was that he was as rubbish at relationships as she was.

For two weeks she'd heard nothing from him. And she'd told herself that was a good thing.

'I'm sorry that lead on my father and Arianna being in Paris turned out to be useless. She really is so lucky to have you.' Polly curled her fingers around his. 'That day at school—I really envied her.'

'For having a brother who came and yelled at her?'

'For having a brother who cared enough to come down to the school and tell her off.'

'I had no idea she was being bullied. I didn't ask the right questions. You have no idea how much I regret that now.'

'You were always there for her. That was the most important

thing.' Feeling disloyal to her father, she gave a quick smile and pulled her hand out of his. 'So, where are we going tonight?'

'It's the opening of a nightclub. Invited guests only.'

As they drew up outside, Polly looked out of the window. 'The Firebird? Oh—I read about this place. It's *seriously* cool. It has a glass dance floor, or something, and the interior looks as though there are flames going up the walls. There's a waiting list of celebrities who want to hire it. And you're invited?'

He gave her a strange look. 'Yes.'

'That's impressive. I read it's almost impossible to get on the guest list. We really wanted to pitch for their advertising just so that we could sneak in and have a look.' Smiling, Polly gave a shiver of excitement and leaned forward in her seat as she saw the crowd gathered. 'I can't wait to tell the others. They're going to be *so* jealous. I had no idea you were a night-club sort of person. I'm discovering all sorts of things about you. Are those photographers?' She shrank slightly. 'Last time I went near a photographer I knocked myself unconscious on his stupid camera.'

'That's why I brought my security team. They can earn their keep.'

'If they're going to take pictures, I'm taking my coat off.'

Damon gave a faint smile. 'Is this going to give me a heart attack?'

'I hope not because I'm not walking through those photographers on my own.' Polly wriggled out of her coat and saw his eyes drop to her cleavage. 'Don't look at me like that. You told me I was allowed to dress up.'

'You look incredible.' His voice husky, he studied her short gold dress and then lifted his gaze to hers. 'You're not wearing Gérard's products tonight?'

'You mentioned dancing so I went for bare legs. Are you going to stare at me or are we going inside?'

It was a heady experience being out in London with Damon. The moment he stepped out of the car the flashbulbs exploded and he held her hand firmly as he walked purposefully towards the entrance of the club. The press pack, kept at bay by his security team, snapped pictures and shouted questions that Damon skilfully deflected.

'I don't see why they're so interested in who you're out with. There are major things going on in the world and all they're interested in is who's in your bed. Crazy.' Keeping her head high, Polly walked with him into the club, waving her arms and walking with a sway in her hips as she heard the seductive pulse of the music. 'I feel like dancing.'

'Good.' Damon gestured to a member of the bar staff and a moment later a bottle of champagne and two glasses appeared. 'We'll have a drink first.'

'Are you one of those men who need alcohol before they hit the dance floor?'

It turned out that he wasn't.

Watching Damon dance was a sensual feast. Every movement made her think of sex, every glance he sent in her direction was a promise of what was to come.

Enjoying herself hugely, Polly let herself go, her body flowing in time to the rhythm, her hair flying around her face as she danced on the shimmering glass floor.

The music and the atmosphere were so infectious that she was still smiling when Damon swept her off the dance floor and back to their private table.

Every few minutes people came up to shake his hand and exchange a few words and Polly wondered why he attracted so much attention wherever he went.

'There are some really famous people here and they're all

coming over to talk to you.' She tapped her champagne glass against his. 'Doukakis for Prime Minister, I say.'

'How much have you drunk?'

'Nowhere near enough. This is the most delicious thing I've ever tasted. In fact the whole experience is super-cool. This place is stunning—' Out of breath, she swallowed a few mouthfuls of champagne and then noticed a couple of minor royals weaving their way towards them. 'I can't curtsey. My dress is too tight—or maybe my bottom is too big. One of the two.' She paused politely while they spoke to Damon and when they finally moved away she sidled closer to him. 'Why is everyone so determined to talk to you?'

'Because I own the place and they're sucking up.' Calm, Damon topped up her glass. 'Do you want to dance again?'

'You own a nightclub?'

'I told you—I believe in diversification. If one part of your business is struggling, another part will be strong. Rules of commerce.'

'But—' Polly looked around her and suddenly realise why everyone had been so deferential when he'd walked in. 'So you're the boss here, too. Everywhere you go, you're the boss. Have you ever *not* been in charge?'

'I spent a crazy night in bed with a woman in Paris recently...' the words were spoken in her ear and his arm was draped across the back of her seat '...and there were definitely a few seconds when I wasn't in charge.'

Her rapid breathing had nothing to do with her exertion on the dance floor and everything to do with the way he made her feel.

'I thought we agreed to forget about that.'

'I changed my mind.'

Her eyes were on his, and then on his mouth. The desire to kiss him was so powerful she almost didn't care that they were in a public place. 'Everyone is looking at us.'

'Then it's probably time to leave.' He rose to his feet and held out his hand to her.

Polly endured the drive home in an agony of sensual anticipation and the moment they closed the door of the penthouse he hauled her against him and divested her of her dress in one slick move that had her gasping.

Equally impatient, she ripped at his shirt, sending buttons flying.

'I want you—' His voice unsteady, Damon pressed her back against the wall and lifted her easily, encouraging her to wrap her thighs around his hips.

She was so ready, so desperate after an evening of watching him on the dance floor, that when she felt him against her she gave a low moan of encouragement and arched her hips to towards him. His fingers gripping her thighs, he entered her with a slow, controlled strength that made her gasp his name. The gasp turned to a sob as she felt him deep inside her and for a moment she stilled, her hand on the sleek skin of his back, her eyes tightly closed as she absorbed the enormity of the pleasure.

'You feel fantastic.' He groaned the words against her mouth and then withdrew and surged into her again, building a rhythm so skilled, so perfect, that her senses caught fire.

Her hands were in his hair, then on his shoulders, and they kissed like savages, biting, licking, feasting as she met each hard thrust with the same frantic desperation. It was primal and out of control, sex at its most basic, a slaking of a physical need that was stronger than both of them.

She came in an exquisite rush of pleasure, her body tightening around his and sending him spinning into the same place.

For what seemed like ages, neither of them moved.

Then he lowered her gently, his forehead against hers. 'Sorry—' his voice was husky '—the bedroom was too far.'

Polly was dizzy with the intensity of it. His lack of control made her feel like a sex goddess. 'No need to apologise—'

'Better get there quickly before it happens again—' He scooped her up again and strode through to the bedroom while Polly reflected briefly on the startling fact that she actually liked it when someone else took control.

Her last coherent thought before he brought his mouth down on hers was that she never wanted it to end.

As dawn broke, Polly sat up carefully, trying not to wake him, but a strong hand shot out and pulled her back down again.

'Where do you think you're going?'

'Back home.'

'No, you're not.' His hand slid into her hair and he kissed her with a slow thoroughness that melted her limbs. 'You're sleeping here. With me.'

She really ought to leave, she thought groggily, but he pulled her into the circle of his arms, trapping her against him.

It felt good, she thought, and the intensity of that feeling terrified her. She'd always avoided this situation, hadn't she? She'd always protected herself from that depth of emotion because she'd seen how fragile relationships were. She'd grown up watching her father's relationships crumble to dust.

But with Damon—

Bombarded with alien feelings that were as terrifying as they were exciting, she stilled in his arms and he turned his head, those dark eyes sharp and astute as he sensed the change in her.

'What's the matter?'

'Nothing.'

'Don't lie to me. I always know when you're keeping something from me. Tell me what's wrong and I'll fix it.' His voice husky and sexy and he slid his hand behind her head and drew her head towards him.

Tell me what's wrong and I'll fix it.

Polly felt a warmth flow through her. It wasn't just that he made her feel like the sexiest woman alive, he was fiercely protective and that was a whole new experience for her.

Was it wrong to enjoy the fact that someone was looking out for her?

His gaze probing, Damon lowered his head to hers, but before he could kiss her his phone buzzed.

Swearing softly, he sighed and rolled onto his back. 'Sorry. Bad timing, but I'd better take this. I'm expecting a call from Athens.' Visibly annoyed at having been disturbed, he reached out and answered it. 'Doukakis…'

Polly lay with her eyes closed, her hand resting on the hard muscle of his chest, struggling to come to terms with the way he made her feel. A night without sleep made his deep voice even huskier and she smiled to herself, thinking that when he spoke in Greek he was even sexier.

Then his voice changed from husky to harsh and he disengaged himself from her grip and launched himself from the bed.

Polly yawned. 'Where are you going?'

'Stay there, and whatever happens don't come out.'

Still lost in her own thoughts, Polly looked at him in a daze, distracted by the sight of his bare back. The swell of smooth male muscle flexed and rippled as he dressed swiftly. He reminded her of a warrior at the peak of fitness, trained and ready to go into battle. Suddenly she wanted to put her arms round him and drag him back to bed. He was the sexiest man she'd ever seen and sex with him was the most breathtakingly exciting experience of her life. 'Come back to bed. Work can wait.'

He didn't look at her. 'I need to see someone. Stay there.'

Hesitating, he turned back to her, planted his arms on the bed and leaned forward to kiss her. 'I'll be back.'

'Mmm…' Still sleepy, Polly smiled against his mouth. 'I'm not sure how to take that. Isn't that a line from *Terminator*?'

He didn't laugh. Instead, he disengaged himself and gently stroked her cheek with his fingers. '*Don't* move. And that's an order.'

Wondering why he was suddenly so serious, she lay still for a moment, floating on a sea of blissful contentment.

And then she heard raised voices coming from the living room.

Raised voices?

Why would there be raised voices?

Concerned, she slid out of bed and wriggled back into the gold dress that lay abandoned on the floor where Damon had thrown it the night before.

The anger in his voice intensified and her curiosity turned to alarm as she hurried through to the living area of the spectacular apartment.

Damon's back was towards her, his feet planted firmly apart in a stance that was blatantly confrontational. Distracted by the display of male power and authority, Polly didn't immediately see who was on the receiving end of his wrath, but as she moved forward, her bare feet making no sound on the wooden floor, the other person finally came into view.

For a moment she was so shocked she couldn't make a sound.

Neither man was aware of her presence, both trapped in their boiling cauldron of mutual animosity.

Feeling the warm threads of her newfound happiness unravel, Polly finally managed to croak out a few words.

'Dad?' Her voice cracked. 'What on earth are you doing here?'

CHAPTER NINE

'I COULD ask you the same question. So the rumours are true.' Her father faced Damon, his expression twisted and ugly. 'Do you have no boundaries? No conscience? It should have been enough for you to take over my company, but no—you had to seal your revenge by seducing my daughter.' His breathing was alarmingly rapid, his hands locked in two white-knuckled fists by his sides.

Revenge?

Polly wanted to move towards her father but her body felt as if it had been encased in cement. She couldn't move. Not once, even for a moment, had it occurred to her that Damon might have seduced her because of her father's relationship with Arianna.

And in that single agonising moment she was finally able to put a name to those alien feelings.

Love.

She'd fallen in love with Damon. Her brain told her it wasn't possible in such a short time but her heart wasn't listening. And maybe it wasn't such a short time, really. He'd always been there, hadn't he? On the fringes of her life. Her friend's big brother.

Terror scraped her skin, sharp as the talons of an eagle, and she stood without speaking, aware of Damon's dangerous mood as he confronted her father.

'You *dare* to come into my home and pretend you care about your daughter? This after several weeks when you haven't bothered to get in touch with anyone?' A look of contempt on his face, Damon took a step towards the older man. 'You are a disgrace. And a coward. You hid rather than face me, but you're here now so stand up and behave like a man. Take responsibilities for your decisions instead of shifting focus onto someone else.'

Still locked in frozen silence, Polly saw her father's face redden.

'Now, you listen to me—' Clearly intimidated by Damon's cold, controlled fury, he momentarily lost some of his bluster. 'I'm no coward. I'm not afraid of you.'

'Well, you should be.' Damon's voice was silky-smooth, his soft tone a thousand times more dangerous than the older man's empty bluster. 'You abandoned your business without thought or care for the future job security of your employees and you did the same with your daughter.'

'I did not abandon her. Polly's not a kid. She's capable of looking after herself.'

'This wasn't a question of cooking herself a meal and getting on with life. You left her to the mercy of those greedy animals you laughingly call a board, all of whom could have been dismissed for misuse of company funds, not to mention sexual harassment, but even worse than that—' the control finally snapped and Damon's voice thickened with anger '—you left her to deal with *me*. By herself. No support from anyone.' Each word thumped into her father like a rock and Polly saw him shrivel.

Torn between her love for two men, she stepped forward, forcing the words through stiff lips. 'Damon, that's enough.'

Damon ignored her. 'Was that your plan? Instead of standing up to me like a man, you left your daughter alone and unprotected in the hope that the lion wouldn't attack? Or have you just completely abdicated your responsibilities as a father?'

'Polly's good at her job. And she's good with people.' But her father's bluster was fading and he glanced warily at Polly. 'You handled him, didn't you?'

Damon exploded, first in Greek and then in English. 'She is twenty-four years old and doesn't have a ruthless bone in her body and yet you abandoned her to be eaten alive by someone of my reputation.'

'I didn't think you'd hurt her.'

Damon's laugh was layered with contempt and disgust. 'You were relying on that. You ran. And you let your defenceless daughter deal with the fall-out. You disgust me. Now, get the hell out of my home.'

'Now, wait a minute—' Her father stumbled over his words. 'Pol isn't defenceless. She's a tough thing.'

'She's had to be! When have you ever stood up for her or helped her? When, in the whole of her life, have you ever been there for her?!'

'I gave her a home when her mother walked out.'

Damon lifted a hand, clenched it into a fist and then lowered it again. '*Don't* say another word,' he warned in a thickened tone. 'Not a word if you want to walk out of here in the same condition you walked in.'

'Stop it!' Finally dragged from her own trauma, Polly stepped between the two men. 'Stop it, both of you! That's enough.' She felt sick inside. So sick that she wanted to crawl into a corner and hide there. Although she knew that everything Damon said was the truth, it didn't stop her loving her father. Life wasn't that simple, was it? 'Dad, where's Arianna?'

'She's back at the house. It's her home now. We're married. We did in secret because we both knew *he*—' he stabbed an accusing finger towards Damon '—would go off the deep end.'

'*Married?*' Polly couldn't hide her dismay and a flash of

real fear chilled her all the way through as she anticipated how Damon would react to that less than welcome news. 'Oh, Dad.'

Her father bristled. 'If I care for a woman, I don't want to just make some sort of sex trophy of her—like him.' He glared at Damon. 'He has plenty of women. He just doesn't marry any of them. What does that say about him?'

'It says that I can tell the difference between lust and love.' Damon spoke through his teeth, his effort to maintain control visible in the pumped muscle of his bare chest and shoulders. 'It says that my decision-making is ruled by my brain and not my testosterone levels.'

Sensing the extreme volatility of his mood, Polly was terrified he was going to lose it. 'I think you'd better leave, Dad,' she said hastily, urging him towards the door.

'Not without you.' Her father dug his heels in and Damon breathed deeply.

'She's staying here. With me. She's mine now.' It was a statement of pure male possession and Polly stilled, hot tears scalding the back of her eyes, knowing that those words were spoken to aggravate her father.

What other explanation was there? Damon had already told her he didn't want a relationship—didn't want commitment or more responsibility. And she knew, as no doubt he did, that nothing would upset her father more than watching her choose Damon over him.

Damon saw their relationship as another weapon to use in the defence of his sister.

'Wait there,' she muttered. 'I'll get dressed.'

Damon turned slowly, an expression of raw incredulity stamped on his spectacularly handsome face as he looked at her. 'You're going with him?'

Polly couldn't breathe. Her mind was a mess and the pain

in her chest felt as though someone had ripped her apart with burning knives. 'I don't have a choice. He's my dad.'

'Of course you have a choice.' Damon's face was unusually pale. '*Theé mou*, tell me that you don't believe any of that garbage he just spouted.'

She hadn't even questioned it.

His animosity towards her father was a living force in the room and the effort not to cry was a physical burning in the back of her throat.

She told herself that even if she were wrong it didn't make a difference to the outcome. The two men she loved were at war with each other and there was no way to make peace. Especially not now that her father had married Arianna. Damon would never forgive him.

Polly felt sick and dizzy and a sense of crawling misery spread through her trembling frame. 'I think it's best if I leave. I—I'll be back at work on Monday, Damon.'

There was a long, agonising silence.

Damon stared at her without speaking. His eyes smouldered dark and his mouth tightened. 'You don't have to give me your work schedule,' he said coldly. 'When you're naked in my bed I'm your lover, not your boss.'

His icy response hurt more than all the words that had been flung around the room and Polly had to physically stop herself from throwing herself at him and trying to undo what had been done.

'He's upsetting you, Pol,' her father said firmly. 'We should just leave.'

It was like separating two stags, she thought numbly. There was never going to be any way of making them get along.

Devastated, she turned her back on both of them and hurried to the bedroom, trying not to remember the incredible happiness she'd felt only moments earlier. Trying to hold it together, she retrieved her shoes and bag and coat and walked back to the living room.

Bracing herself for another desperately upsetting encounter with Damon, she saw only her father.

'Where's Damon?'

'He's gone. Gave me a look and walked out.' Her father cast a nervous look around the apartment. 'The guy's unstable. You're well rid of him, Pol. Let's get out of here.'

Arriving back at her own home, Polly felt numb with misery. She just wanted to retreat to her room but she knew there was no hope of that.

Oblivious to her agony, her father was chatting excitedly, telling her about his wedding in the Caribbean.

She felt as though she were trapped in a recurring cycle.

Another woman. Another relationship.

She should have been used to it by now, but this time it felt different and not just because Arianna was her friend.

'Are you mad with me, Pol?' Arianna hovered anxiously as Polly walked into the house with her father. 'It's going to be seriously weird being your stepmother, but once we get over that is everything going to be cool between us? I mean, I know you must be mad with Damon, but that's just the way he is. You know that, right? And we don't have to see that much of him.'

That statement depressed her more than anything else that had been said so far. 'I'm working for him,' Polly said flatly. 'I have to see him.'

'You can get another job,' her father said cheerfully, sliding his arm around Arianna and kissing her on the cheek. 'I'm thinking of setting up again. I'll employ you.'

'No, thanks.' Polly found that she couldn't look at Arianna without thinking of Damon. 'I like the job I have now. Damon is an inspirational boss.'

Her father looked affronted. 'Well, he's good with numbers, that's true, and he's certainly—'

'Dad, just—' Teetering on the edge of an emotional explosion, Polly held up her hand. 'Just don't say anything else, OK? This whole thing could have gone a completely different way. Everyone could have been made redundant and—' She broke off, too exhausted to fight with anyone. 'Never mind.'

Arianna walked over and gave her a hug. 'You've had a terrible few weeks. Believe me, no one knows better than me what it's like having Damon breathing down your neck, checking on everything you're doing. He does it because he's a complete and utter control freak.'

Polly snapped. 'Actually, he does it because he cares. He cares about *you*—' The fury shook her and she pushed her astonished friend away. 'He thinks about your welfare and he cares whether you're happy. He sees it as his role to protect you and he's made enormous personal sacrifices to care for you and make sure that you grew up with family and not a bunch of strangers. So maybe you could start seeing things from his point of view for a change. Why the hell didn't you phone him?! The guy has been worried sick!'

'Why are you defending him?' Astonished, Arianna exchanged uncertain looks with her new husband. 'Polly—'

'I'm going upstairs to do some work.' Polly turned away, seriously shaken by the intensity of her desire to defend Damon from attack. She would have thrown herself in front of a moving vehicle to protect him from harm. 'I have a job to do and I intend to keep it, no matter what shambles my personal life is in.' She knew that no matter what had happened between them there was no way that Damon would allow the personal to overtake the professional. She knew that her job was safe.

In the privacy of her bedroom, she locked the door and then

flung herself on her bed, feeling something close to desperate. The emptiness inside her was a big dark hole.

It was hard to believe that it was only yesterday she'd been celebrating a promotion and the achievement of a lifetime ambition—to do a business degree—and now—

Now she felt nothing but a sense of profound loss.

All the happiness had been sucked out of her.

Polly turned her head and looked at the prospectus that lay by her bed but somehow today it didn't have the power to lift her spirits as it had the day before.

Frightened by how bad she felt, she tried to reason with herself.

She'd done everything she'd set out to do.

No one was going to be fired. Thanks to Gérard, money and business was flowing into the company. Damon was finally aware of her true role in the company.

She should feel proud. Relieved.

But suddenly none of that seemed important.

Instead of feeling as if she'd won, she felt as if she'd lost. Everything.

The temptation to go off sick on Monday was huge.

'Don't go in,' her father urged as Polly grabbed her BlackBerry and slipped it in her bag. 'Just stay at home. Switch your phone off.'

'I have a job, Dad. Responsibilities.' She gave him a pointed look and he had the grace to colour. 'We've just won a massive account and I'm in charge of it. Excuse me. I'm going to be late.'

She travelled to work by her usual route, feeling as though she had lead weights attached to her feet.

Maybe Damon would be in meetings all day. Or perhaps he

would have found a reason to travel to New York or Athens. She didn't know which would be worse—seeing him or not seeing him.

The moment she walked onto her floor she sensed something different in the atmosphere.

'Morning, Polly,' Debbie said cheerfully. 'Coffee and muffin on your desk.'

Polly decided that to confess that she wasn't hungry would simply invite questions, so she just smiled. 'Thanks. I'm going to have a team meeting at eleven to discuss the High Kick Hosiery account. Can you summon the troops?'

'Sure, but I just took a call for you—could you pop down to the tenth floor. Accounts.'

Polly put her bag down on her desk. 'Why?'

'No idea. I just follow orders. And there are enough of them flying around here.' With that enigmatic statement Debbie strolled off, leaving Polly with the distinct feeling that something was going on.

Did they all know what had happened between her and Damon?

The thought horrified her and suddenly escaping to the accounts floor seemed like a good idea.

Pushing open the doors, she walked onto the tenth floor and stopped in astonishment.

The last time she'd been down here it had been as stark and businesslike as the rest of the Doukakis office space. Now, it had been transformed into a carbon copy of her own floor. Photographs had appeared on desks, along with small personal items. Plants clustered in a central point, bringing a soothing, relaxing quality to the huge area.

Astonished, Polly turned to the woman nearest to her. 'Er—what happened here?'

'Haven't you seen the e-mail?' Grinning, the woman tapped

a few keys on her machine and brought up an e-mail. 'Here we are. It came right from the top. *"Personalising the office".'*

Polly leaned forward and read over her shoulder:

With immediate effect the hot desk system that we have operated for the past year will cease. Employees are encouraged to personalise their office space in any way that they believe will make them more productive. DD

'Isn't it great?' The woman was beaming. 'I can't tell you how tired I was of moving from one desk to another. I had to keep my books in the boot of my car. Ridiculous. I don't know who got him to change his mind but they're a genius.'

Polly managed a smile. 'Right. Great.'

What was going on?

Puzzled, she looked around, trying to absorb the magnitude of the change, but before she could ask any more questions her phone buzzed. It was Jenny, Damon's PA.

Cautiously, she answered it. 'Hi, Jenny.'

'The boss wants to talk to you, Polly. His office. Five minutes.'

Her hand shaking, Polly put the phone back in her pocket and the woman looked at her expectantly.

'Was there someone you wanted to see?'

Polly took a last look at the transformed office. 'No,' she croaked. 'I think I just saw it.'

But she didn't understand it.

Smoothing her dress, she stepped in the lift and felt sicker and sicker as it rose smoothly to the executive floor. As soon as she walked out Jenny waved her towards the office, a huge smile on her face.

'He's waiting for you. I have orders to make sure you're not disturbed.'

'That sounds ominous.' Slowly, Polly walked forward and tapped on the door. Hearing his voice, she took a deep breath and walked into the room.

Damon sat behind his desk, talking on the phone. When he saw her he beckoned her in and gestured to the chair.

Feeling ridiculously self-conscious, she slid into the chair—and then noticed the fish tank on his desk.

Her mouth fell open.

Fish?

Wondering if she were seeing things, she blinked, but the fish remained.

Damon ended the call. 'You're wearing your flamingo-pink tights. Good. They suit you.'

Polly was still staring at the tank on his desk. 'You bought fish.'

A faint smile touched his mouth. 'Someone told me they were an excellent addition to the office environment. Relaxing. I'm feeling tense at the moment so I thought I'd give it a try.'

Her heart started to pound and she wanted to ask why he was feeling tense. 'I saw your memo.'

'Apparently I've gone up ten points in the popularity stakes,' he drawled. 'You were right. People do like personal things around them in the office. It's just one of lots of changes I'll be making.'

She licked her lips. 'Oh.'

'Now you're supposed to ask me what the others are.'

The comment was so typical of Damon that normally she would have laughed, but today she just couldn't make the sound. 'What are the others?'

'I'm making pink tights compulsory.'

Polly flushed, and he watched her for a long moment and then rose to his feet.

'The fact that you can't even raise a smile tells me that

you're as miserably unhappy about this whole situation as I am. That's all I wanted to know.' He walked round his desk and hauled her to her feet in a decisive movement that left no room for protest. 'I owe you an apology. I lost my temper with your father and I shouldn't have done.'

'I don't blame you for that,' Polly muttered. 'In fact I lost it with him myself.'

'I shouldn't have put you in the position of making you choose between us.' A wry smile touched his mouth. 'I didn't think for a moment that you'd walk out on me. You have a way of cutting a guy down to size very quickly.'

'Damon, I really don't want to—'

'Talk about this. I know.' He took her face in his hands. 'But you're going to. I know how afraid you are of relationships, Polly. Your life has been like a car park, with a constant stream of people coming and going. It's not rocket science to deduce that you're going to have commitment issues. That's why I forgive you for thinking the worst of me on Friday.'

'Forgive you?'

'Yes. Forgive you.' He bent his head and kissed her mouth gently. 'It's not very flattering when the woman you love is so ready to believe that you took her to bed out of an impulse to get revenge on her father. That hurt.'

Polly stilled, suddenly unable to breathe. 'Damon?'

'I love you.' He spoke the words softly but his eyes were full of passion and heat. 'I've spent my whole life making sure I didn't fall in love. Then I met you again and suddenly I didn't have a choice.'

The words sank slowly into her brain. 'You told me you were never going to let that happen.'

'Which means you've proved once again that I'm nowhere near as in control of things as I like to think.' He hesitated. 'You're right that I was scared of being responsible for someone else's happiness. I saw what happened when my father thought he'd let everyone down. I had Arianna, all these employees—I didn't want anyone else. Until you came back into my life. I love you more than I ever thought it possible to love someone.'

The happiness was so intense it was blinding. 'Truly?'

'I told your father that you're mine now.'

'I assumed you were trying to wind him up.'

'I was telling the truth, but I don't blame you for questioning my motives. It's true that I'd do anything to protect Arianna, but this isn't about my sister any more. It's about us.'

'Us.' Polly whispered the word. 'I've never been an "us". I'm not sure I'll be any good at it.'

'We'll learn together. I'm already learning fast,' he assured her. 'I've turned my company upside down. From now on we're following the Polly Prince code of office management. And as for the rest of it—I know it breaks every rule, but I want us to be together.'

'But—'

'I know you're scared. I know you're thinking that your father has just married for the fifth time and that relationships can't last, but ours can and will—' He lowered his mouth to hers and kissed her, his mouth stirring up the fire inside her. 'Look at me and tell me that you don't think we'll still be together in fifty years.'

Polly looked at him, her heart aching and her eyes swimming. 'I want to be. I love you, too. Oh, God, I can't believe I'm saying that.'

'You've no idea how relieved I am to hear you say it.' The corner of his mouth tilted and he reached into his pocket and withdrew a box. 'I bought this for you. I want you to wear it always. Hopefully whenever the thought of being an "us" scares you, you can look at it and be reminded of how much I love you.' He flipped the box open and withdrew a huge, sparkling diamond ring and Polly felt as if her whole heart had been opened and exposed.

Tears fell and landed on his hand. 'It's beautiful, but I can't wear it. How can I? You say that this is just about us, but it isn't. It can't be.' It all seemed hopeless to her. The obstacles too big. 'I love my father, Damon. I know he behaves like a total idiot sometimes and, yes, he's careless, but that's just the way he is—' She wiped her tears on her sleeve. 'I'm the first to admit that he's pretty crap at a lot of things, but he was there. And now you hate him, and he's married your sister, and we can't be together with you hating him—' Hiccuping, she heard her words tumble together, and Damon gave a low curse and gathered her against him.

'*Don't* cry. I never want to see you cry. We'll work things out with your father, I promise.'

'I don't want to be in a position where I'm always having to take sides and choose.'

'You won't be,' he vowed. 'You have my word on that. I've already been to see your father. We managed to talk without killing each other so that's a good start.'

Polly sniffed. 'You've seen him?'

'This morning. After you left for work. My sister apologised to me.'

'She did?'

'Apparently you told her a few truths. She took them on board and suddenly she feels very guilty that she's caused me so much worry.' He wrapped his arms around her and held her close. 'When we were in the boardroom that day you told me I was over-protective and you were right.'

'No, I was wrong. You're brilliant and Arianna is lucky.'

'But the sense of responsibility I felt towards Arianna prevented me from letting her spread her wings. I couldn't bear the thought of anything happening to her. I'd promised myself that I was going to protect her and I never questioned that as time went on.'

'And you did an amazing job.'

'I want to stop thinking about them and think about us.' He slid his fingers gently over her cheek, wiping away her tears. 'Don't think about our families—that will be fine, I promise you. The decision about our future rests entirely on whether you can bring yourself to spend the rest of your life with me.'

'Wow. Well—' As happiness finally flowed through her, Polly's voice cracked. 'That sounds pretty tough.'

'You're *going* to marry me,' Damon breathed, 'and, unlike your father and Arianna, we're going to have a huge wedding so that we can invite all the people who have worked with you for so long, otherwise there will be a mass walk-out.'

Unable to believe that this was happening, Polly flung her arms round his neck. 'I love you *so* much. It's terrifying. Really, seriously scary.'

Damon held her close. 'Then it's a good thing that you're brave. You can meet terror head-on, the way you did that morning in the boardroom when you stalked in wearing those sexy boots, looking as if you wanted to knife me.'

'Did I ever tell you that you looked extremely hot in that suit?'

His laugh was husky as he eased her away just enough for him to see her face. 'You think I looked hot in my suit? How hot?'

Polly gave a slow smile and slid her hands down his back. 'Red-hot. Scorching.'

'In that case—I know you have a powerful work ethic, but you're about to be unexpectedly unavailable for the next hour.' Ignoring her gasp of shock, he scooped her into his arms and strode out of the office. 'Jenny, hold my calls.'

Jenny didn't bother hiding her smile. 'Yes, Mr Doukakis.'

Mortified, Polly hid her face in Damon's shoulder. 'This is *so* embarrassing. And I have work to do. I don't want everyone to think I'm a slacker.'

'I'm giving you permission to take the next hour off, Miss Prince.' Still holding her, he hit the lift button with his elbow and the doors closed.

Laughing, overwhelmed by happiness, Polly kissed him. 'Whatever you say,' she said happily. 'You're the boss.'

Coming Next Month

from **Harlequin Presents® EXTRA.** Available October 11, 2011.

#169 IN WANT OF A WIFE?
Cathy Williams
The Powerful and the Pure

#170 THE RETURN OF THE STRANGER
Kate Walker
The Powerful and the Pure

#171 THE S BEFORE EX
Mira Lyn Kelly
Tabloid Scandals

#172 SEX, GOSSIP AND ROCK & ROLL
Nicola Marsh
Tabloid Scandals

Coming Next Month

from **Harlequin Presents®.** Available October 25, 2011.

#3023 THE MOST COVETED PRIZE
Penny Jordan
Russian Rivals

#3024 THE MAN WITH THE MONEY
Lynn Raye Harris
The Notorious Wolfes

#3025 JEWEL IN HIS CROWN
Lynne Graham

#3026 THE ICE PRINCE
Sandra Marton
The Orsini Brides

#3027 THE PRICE OF SCANDAL
Kim Lawrence

#3028 A ROYAL ENGAGEMENT
Trish Morey and Caitlin Crews

**Visit www.HarlequinInsideRomance.com
for more information on upcoming titles!**

REQUEST YOUR FREE BOOKS!

2 FREE NOVELS PLUS
2 FREE GIFTS!

Harlequin® Special Edition® is thrilled to present a new installment in **USA TODAY** *bestselling author RaeAnne Thayne's reader-favorite miniseries,* **THE COWBOYS OF COLD CREEK.**

Join the excitement as we meet the Bowmans—four siblings who lost their parents but keep family ties alive in Pine Gulch. First up is Trace. Only two things get under this rugged lawman's skin: beautiful women and secrets. And in Rebecca Parsons, he finds both!

Read on for a sneak peek of **CHRISTMAS IN COLD CREEK.** *Available November 2011 from Harlequin® Special Edition®.*

On impulse, he unfolded himself from the bar stool. "Need a hand?"

"Thank you! I…" She lifted her gaze from the floor to his jeans and then raised her eyes. When she identified him her hazel eyes turned from grateful to unfriendly and cold, as if he'd somehow thrown the broken glasses at her head.

He also thought he saw a glimmer of panic in those interesting depths, which instantly stirred his curiosity like cream swirling through coffee.

"I've got it, Officer. Thank you." Her voice was several degrees colder than the whirl of sleet outside the windows.

Despite her protests, he knelt down beside her and began to pick up shards of broken glass. "No problem. Those trays can be slippery."

This close, he picked up the scent of her, something fresh and flowery that made him think of a mountain meadow on a July afternoon. She had a soft, lush mouth and for one brief, insane moment, he wanted to push aside that stray lock of hair slipping from her ponytail and taste her. Apparently he needed to spend a lot less time working and a great deal *more* time recreating with the opposite sex if he could have sudden random fantasies about a woman he wasn't even inclined to like, pretty or not.

"I'm Trace Bowman. You must be new in town."

She didn't answer immediately and he could almost see the wheels turning in her head. Why the hesitancy? And why that little hint of unease he could see clouding the edge of her gaze? His presence was obviously making her uncomfortable and Trace couldn't help wondering why.

"Yes. We've been here a few weeks."

"Well, I'm just up the road about four lots, in the white house with the cedar shake roof, if you or your daughter need anything." He smiled at her as he picked up the last shard of glass and set it on her tray.

Definitely a story there, he thought as she hurried away. He just might need to dig a little into her background to find out why someone with fine clothes and nice jewelry, and who so obviously didn't have experience as a waitress, would be here slinging hash at The Gulch. Was she running away from someone? A bad marriage?

So…Rebecca Parsons. Not Becky. An intriguing woman. It had been a long time since one of those had crossed his path here in Pine Gulch.

Trace won't rest until he finds out Rebecca's secret, but will he still have that same attraction to her once he does? Find out in CHRISTMAS IN COLD CREEK. Available November 2011 from Harlequin® Special Edition®.

brings you

USA TODAY Bestselling Author

Penny Jordan

Part of the new miniseries

RUSSIAN RIVALS

*Demidov vs. Androvonov—let the most
merciless of men win...*

Kiryl Androvonov

The Russian oligarch has one rival: billionaire
Vasilii Demidov. Luckily, Vasilii has an Achilles' heel—his
younger, overprotected, beautiful half sister, Alena...

Vasilii Demidov

After losing his sister to his bitter rival, Vasilii is far too
cynical to ever trust a woman, not even his secretary Laura.
Never did she expect to be at the ruthless Russian's mercy....

The rivalry begins in...

THE MOST COVETED PRIZE—November
THE POWER OF VASILII—December

**Available wherever
Harlequin Presents® books are sold.**

www.Harlequin.com

HP13023

Harlequin®

Desire

ALWAYS POWERFUL, PASSIONATE AND PROVOCATIVE.

NEW YORK TIMES AND *USA TODAY*
BESTSELLING AUTHOR

BRENDA JACKSON

**PRESENTS A BRAND-NEW TALE
OF SEDUCTION**

TEMPTATION

TEXAS CATTLEMAN'S CLUB: THE SHOWDOWN

Millionaire security expert and rancher Zeke Travers
always separates emotion from work. Until a case
leads him to Sheila Hopkins—and the immediate,
scorching heat that leaped between them. Suddenly,
Zeke is tempted to break the rules. And it's only a
matter of time before he gives in....

Available November wherever books are sold.